"You've been lucky for me,"
Max stated.

"We just unearthed three more fossils."

"More bones?" Rikki questioned with apprehension. "Do you think there might be a whole dinosaur down there?"

"There might be. I guess that puts us at odds, doesn't it? I'm hoping for a whole dinosaur, and you're hoping that the rest of him is anywhere but here."

He made her feel as if she was taking away a deprived child's only Christmas present. "It's just that I have a ranch to run. If you stay here, disrupting everything, who knows when things will get back to normal?"

"Is it the work that's disrupting you, or your reaction to me?" Max countered.

Dear Reader,

Whether it's a vacation fling in some far-off land, or falling for the guy next door, there's something irresistible about summer romance. This month, we have an irresistible lineup for you, ranging from sunny to sizzling.

We continue our FABULOUS FATHERS series with *Accidental Dad* by Anne Peters. Gerald Marsden is not interested in being tied down! But once he finds himself the temporary father of a lonely boy, *and* the temporary husband of his lovely landlady, Gerald wonders if he might not actually enjoy a permanent role as "family man."

Marie Ferrarella, one of your favorite authors, brings us a heroine who's determined to settle down—but not with a man who's always rushing off to another archaeological site! However, when Max's latest find shows up *In Her Own Backyard,* Rikki makes some delightful discoveries of her own....

The popular Phyllis Halldorson returns to Silhouette Romance for a special story about reunited lovers who must learn to trust again, in *More Than You Know.* Kasey Michaels brings her bright and humorous style to a story of love at long distance in the enchanting *Marriage in a Suitcase.*

Rounding out July are two stories that simmer with passion and deception—*The Man Behind the Magic* by Kristina Logan and *Almost Innocent* by Kate Bradley.

In the months to come, look for more titles by your favorite authors—including Diana Palmer, Elizabeth August, Suzanne Carey, Carla Cassidy and many, many more!

Happy reading!

Anne Canadeo
Senior Editor

IN HER OWN
BACKYARD

Marie Ferrarella

Silhouette
ROMANCE™
Published by Silhouette Books New York
America's Publisher of Contemporary Romance

To Mary Ann Johnston,
who also exchanged one
madding crowd for another

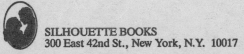

SILHOUETTE BOOKS
300 East 42nd St., New York, N.Y. 10017

IN HER OWN BACKYARD

Copyright © 1993 by Marie Rydzynski-Ferrarella

ISBN: 0-373-08947-3

First Silhouette Books printing July 1993

Printed in the U.S.A.

MARIE FERRARELLA

was born in Europe, raised in New York City and now lives in Southern California. She describes herself as the tired mother of two overenergetic children and the contented wife of one wonderful man. She is thrilled to be following her dream of writing full-time.

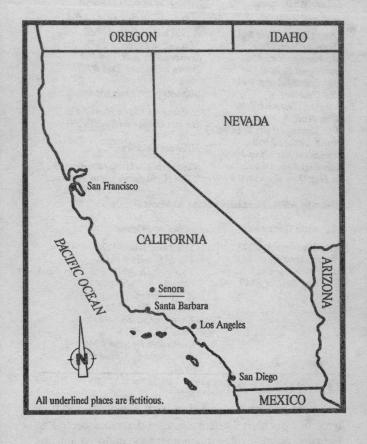

OREGON

IDAHO

NEVADA

• San Francisco

CALIFORNIA

PACIFIC OCEAN

ARIZONA

N

• Senora
Santa Barbara
• Los Angeles

• San Diego

All underlined places are fictitious.

MEXICO

Chapter One

Hers.

As far as the eye could see. It was all hers. No midtown traffic polluting the air and jangling her nerves. No suitcases to live out of or planes to catch. Just peace and tranquillity. Nature at its very best. It was a little piece of heaven, and it was hers.

Roots. She had finally put down roots.

Erikka McGuire leaned back in her cushioned swivel chair and let a contented sigh escape her lips. She had picked this room as her den because of the magnificent view. She was lucky, and she knew it. It hadn't been easy getting here. But then, maybe if it had been, the final victory might not have felt as special.

An urgent knock on her front door interrupted her mental meanderings.

"It's open," she called out. There was no need for locked doors in Senora. Another plus, she thought. She liked the luxury of trusting people. She also liked the luxury of not tripping over them if she so chose.

Turning slightly in her chair, she looked toward the doorway in time to see the stocky figure of Roger Whitecastle shuffle through the other room. Dressed in a red work shirt and sagging, faded jeans, he had a permanently worn, dusty appearance about him. An apt one, Rikki thought, considering his vocation. The expression on his face was not a happy one as he ran his wide hand through his full head of yellow-white hair. She wondered what was wrong this time. He had already registered several complaints since he had come to work for her.

"Doc, I think we got trouble."

The contractor she had hired to build a new, larger stable was a man of few words. Rikki thought she would extract a few more before she allowed herself to worry. "Define trouble, Mr. Whitecastle."

Small, steely-blue eyes bored into hers. "One of my boys found a bone."

Rikki pushed herself away from her desk and stood up. This, for a change, was something different. "What kind of a bone, Mr. Whitecastle? Human?"

The sun-creased face didn't change expression. "I can't rightly say."

She was already out the door, striding quickly ahead of him. It was probably nothing, she told herself, refusing to become concerned too soon. She had been planning to build a larger stable from the very first day she had bought the property. She wasn't about to change her plans. Undoubtedly the workers had unearthed some animal or other that time had long since forgotten. There was no unsolved murder in the vicinity. If there had been, the local gossips would have gleefully filled her in before her moving van had even driven out of sight.

The foundation for the new stable was a short walk from the house. Work on it had begun barely two days ago. There was a horse auction coming up near Santa Barbara in six weeks, and Rikki had hoped to have the stable completed by then so she could have the additional horses she was planning on purchasing shipped very quickly. With any luck, this discovery wouldn't put a crimp in her plans.

The six men who Roger Whitecastle employed were all related to him in one way or another. He told her he liked to keep things in the family. That was the way Senora was, she had discovered, tight family units. Rikki was still trying to find her place.

The men were all standing in an idle ring around the hole they had been digging. It was late June, and the air was dry, but four of the men had stripped off their shirts, their muscular torsos glistening with perspiration. As Rikki neared, they all straightened ever so slightly, stallions preening for a thoroughbred mare.

She felt their eyes all turn toward her as she approached. She still felt like a newcomer after almost a year, only half fitting into the scheme of things. It was much slower going than she had anticipated. That she was twenty-eight, single and attractive hadn't helped her nearly as much as the fact that she was an experienced veterinarian and Doc Wilson had chosen this year to retire. Having witnessed her work, he had personally recommended her to the ranchers in the area before he had left. It had helped. Some. Only time and patience, she knew, would do the rest.

Rikki slid down into the hole on her rear, ignoring the offered hand of one of the men. She turned, waiting for

Whitecastle to join her. The old man grunted as he followed suit. Rikki dusted off her jeans and then turned to him. "Where is it?"

He motioned her over to a section on the left. Leading the way, he stopped and tapped his boot on a large bone sticking up out of the ground.

Rikki squatted down and examined it closely. It looked like something a dog had begun to bury, then forgotten about. A very large dog.

"Looks too thick to be human." She touched it gingerly with her fingers but didn't pick it up, wondering what sort of animal it had belonged to.

Whitecastle blew his nose in a huge handkerchief and then stuffed it into his back pocket. It didn't go in easily. "I've sent Billy for the sheriff."

Billy was Whitecastle's youngest son, and from what Rikki had witnessed of his work habits, he was probably relieved at the reprieve. Whatever his feelings, Rikki's weren't too happy about Whitecastle's decision. She stood up and surveyed the surrounding area. There was so much work to be done. "Is that really necessary? I can see that the bone doesn't belong to a hu—"

Whitecastle tugged at the waistband of his pants, a struggle that he waged both unsuccessfully and constantly. "I've found that it's best to do things by the book. The sheriff likes to know about these things."

The sheriff, Rikki thought, had precious little to occupy himself with as it was. And she was in a hurry. But she could tell by the set of the contractor's jaw that neither he nor his men were going to move another shovelful of dirt until Sheriff Pete Beamish told them that it was all right to go ahead.

Knowing when she was outnumbered, Rikki nodded wearily. "Call me when he gets here."

This time, when one of the men offered her a hand, she grasped it and allowed him to pull her up, then offered him a smile of thanks, scarcely seeing him.

Oh well, she thought as she walked back to the house. What was a few hours' delay? The sheriff was an intelligent man. He would see that the bone was far too thick to belong to a human skeleton. And then everything would get back to normal.

She grinned at the flash of impatience she had felt. An obvious carryover from the life she had led while growing up. "You can take the woman out of the city," she murmured as she went into the house, "but you can't take the city out of the woman."

The sheriff arrived at her house an hour later. Together they went back to where the digging had stopped. Wearing a thoughtful expression, the thin, older man did a lot of staring and prodding with the toe of his boot before he agreed with Rikki's observation that the bone didn't appear to belong to someone who had been gruesomely murdered and buried on her property.

"Nope," he pronounced, "it sure isn't human."

Rikki smiled, grateful that the matter had been settled. She began to climb out of the hole. "Fine, then the men can get back to work."

There was a long pause behind her. Rikki turned around and looked at the sheriff expectantly.

Pete shook his head solemnly. "'Fraid not."

Rikki was sure she wasn't hearing him correctly. "Why not?"

"Why don't we get back on level ground?" he suggested.

Annoyed by what she felt was a play for drama on the sheriff's part, Rikki climbed out and waited for the man to join her. They were alone, except for Whitecastle. The others had retreated to the truck to take an early, extended lunch.

"Okay." Rikki attempted to curb the impatient tone in her voice. "Why can't the men get back to work?"

The sheriff pushed his broad-brimmed hat onto the back of his head. Words flowed slowly when he spoke. "Because I'm going to have to report it."

"To who?"

"The museum."

Rikki narrowed her eyes. She'd been afraid of this. As a professional in the medical field, she could appreciate the problem. As a rancher who had horses coming and nowhere to put them, she could not. "The museum? What museum? And why?"

Pete gave her a tolerant smile, as if she were a child who needed to be educated. She could tell that he was thoroughly enjoying this. "If I were to make a guess, I'd say that was an old bone, maybe even a dinosaur bone. Need one of them scientists to come out and take a look."

"Dinosaur?" she echoed halfheartedly.

"Maybe."

The sheriff might have looked and sounded like someone's idea of a hayseed, but Rikki knew better. Beneath the drawl and laid-back facade was a well-educated, sharp man who couldn't be easily swayed once he had made up his mind. And he had obviously made up his mind about this.

Rikki sighed, ran her hand through dark brown hair she had always felt was too thick and looked at him. "How long will that take?"

"Depends on when they can send a man out."

Rikki shut her eyes and muttered under her breath. She had moved here to get away from the fast pace of life in a large city. But slow as molasses wasn't exactly her speed, either. "And when do you think that might be?"

Pete had removed his hat and was scratching the bald patch on his head. "Maybe a week." He paused. "Maybe more."

She didn't have a week. The auction wasn't that far off. But apparently she didn't have much of a choice in the matter. And she wanted to get along with the people in this community. She didn't relish being branded a troublemaker as well as a newcomer. Impressions like that, she knew, were hard to erase. "Do whatever you have to, Sheriff."

"Thanks, Doc, I usually do."

Taking a fortifying breath, she aimed eyes that were as close to violet as humanly possible at the weather-beaten face of the man standing next to the sheriff. "Mr. Whitecastle, we have to have a little talk."

"About what?" he asked suspiciously.

She looked at the large, gaping hole that *should* have been the foundation of her stable. Flexibility had always been a byword with her. "About moving the site of the stable."

Whitecastle tugged at the belt that was straining valiantly against his huge belly. "It's gonna cost you."

Rikki found that she couldn't help grinning at the solemn way he had made his revelation. "I never doubted it for a moment."

Whitecastle brightened at the prospect of more money. "Why don't you and I discuss it over some cool lemonade? Unless—" he eyed her hopefully "—you've got something stronger?"

It was the longest sentence she had heard him utter to date. "Beer all right with you?"

"Beer's just fine with me."

Rikki had a huge suspicion she knew just how Whitecastle's wide waistline had come into being.

The sound of the ringing phone emerging from beneath the clutter on his desk broke the silence that enshrouded the musty back room where David Maxwell made his office. He rubbed his forehead before he picked up the phone on the third ring. Being indoors for any length of time always seemed to bring on a headache. This headache was approximately nine months old.

"Professor Maxwell."

"Max?" Sheriff Beamish laughed warmly. "This is Sheriff Beamish. How are you?"

Max was surprised to hear from the man. He had known Pete Beamish for twenty-five of his thirty-two years, ever since he had gone to school with the sheriff's son, Allen. But that didn't explain why the sheriff would suddenly call him out of the blue.

"I'm fine, Sheriff. How's Allen? I haven't heard from him in a while."

"Made me a grandfather again."

"That's terrific. Tell him I said hello. So—" he cradled the phone against his ear with his shoulder as he tried to stack a few papers into order "—what can I do for you?"

"It's more of a matter of what I can do for you." There was a pregnant pause. Max remembered the older man's taste for suspense. "I think I've got something here that might interest you."

Max let the papers drop and took the receiver into his hand. "Oh?"

"A construction crew was digging the foundations for a stable this morning and came upon a bone."

Max slid to the edge of his chair. "What kind of a bone?"

Pete chuckled. "That's your department, not mine. But one thing I can tell you, it isn't human."

Max knew the man wouldn't be calling if they had unearthed something as simple as a farm animal's bones. "Dinosaur?"

"Could be. Bigger than anything I've ever seen, at any rate." The tone was that of a man well pleased with himself. "How soon can you get here?"

Max told himself not to get excited. It was probably a false alarm. But he felt an enthusiasm surging through him that hadn't been there a moment ago. "Tomorrow morning suit you?"

Pete chuckled. "Not much doing at the museum these days?"

Max stretched. The chair felt confining. The whole office felt confining. "I'm not a paper pusher, Sheriff. I like being out in the open, fossil hunting."

"Yeah, I remember."

"Not that I'm complaining, mind you, but they've had me behind this stupid desk for nine months now. I figure I've given them enough of the bright young paleontologist at work. It's time for me to get back into the thick of things." Mentally he was already packing his belongings and making plans. It seemed incredible to him that the sleepy little town he had longed to leave might actually contain something that had always been his heart's desire.

"I'll stop by your office and you can give me directions."

"Sure, and Max?"

"Yeah?"

"The property belongs to a lady vet."

The news surprised him. "What happened to Doc Wilson?" He remembered the old, white-haired man who had looked gnarled to him even as a young boy.

"He retired."

"Too bad. I liked him."

Max could hear the smile in the sheriff's voice. "You'll like her even better."

"Just so long as she's got something interesting for me." Max's eyes rested on the poster on the back of his door. It depicted a huge *Tyrannosaurus rex*. To be part of finding something like that... He told himself he was dreaming again.

"That depends on how you play your cards." The sheriff chuckled at his own joke. "See you tomorrow."

"Count on it."

Max let the phone slip from his fingers back into the cradle. He didn't want to get excited, but he was. He exercised caution when on a site, but the possibility of there *being* a site filled him with euphoria. Working out in the field was what he liked best about his profession. He liked to think of himself as a scientific detective, hunting for clues to a life long since past, except that the clues he looked for took the form of fossils. He had found quite a few of those, but never anything of major proportions.

Absently he fingered the small bronze *Apatosaurus* statue on his desk as his mind drifted. Maybe this time he would strike the mother lode. The last three excavations had turned up only a few miscellaneous fossils and nothing more. He wanted to have something to sink his teeth into, something to *do*. Being an assistant curator at the museum was all well and good and looked impressive on a letter, but he wasn't interested in prestige or position. He just wanted the challenge, the exhilaration, of coming in contact with a piece of history that time had tried to hide from the world.

More than anything, he thought with a silent laugh, he wanted his own dinosaur.

Max was still trying to check his growing enthusiasm as he drove his Land Rover onto Rikki's property the next afternoon. Having first checked in with the sheriff, Max had gotten the appropriate directions and made his way to the ranch.

He had forgotten how pretty this country was and how much he missed it. There was no longer any family left for him to visit, but the land had a familiar feel to it that couldn't be usurped by the modern apartment he now called home. In his own way, he knew he was a man of the earth and always would be.

By the time he reached the doorstep of the rambling, two-story ranch house where Rikki lived, his excitement was barely restrained.

Rikki heard the sharp, staccato knock on her front door from her upstairs bedroom. Abandoning her search for an elusive medical book, she called out, "Coming," and then ran down the stairs.

"Always something," she said to herself, feeling uncustomarily out of sorts. Whitecastle and his crew still hadn't gotten started on the new site.

She threw open the door, then stopped short. The first thing she saw was shoulders. Doorjamb-to-doorjamb shoulders. Obviously this man was no stranger to work, she assessed. A wrangler, maybe, looking for a job. It wasn't uncommon in the area. And with her only hand away, she could use the help.

She let her eyes trail up to his face. Not a handsome face, she decided, but rugged, manly. Open. A face with character. The sandy hair that the wind was ruffling was cut a little long. She caught herself smiling.

Aware that she hadn't said anything, Rikki cleared her throat. "Can I help you?"

"Are you Dr. McGuire?" It seemed a little strange to Max calling someone so young and slender "Doctor." She looked no older than about twenty-two, he judged. Maybe she was Erikka McGuire's younger sister or daughter. The sheriff hadn't bothered describing the woman. He had merely smiled—broadly.

"Yes?" From the confident way he held himself, Rikki decided that he wasn't looking for work. Maybe he was a ranch hand sent by one of the other ranchers with an ailing animal, she thought. That was hopeful. Business had been very slow lately. The area seemed to have unusually healthy livestock.

"I've come to see your bone."

Rikki blinked. "Excuse me?"

Max grinned. "I'm sorry, I'm getting ahead of myself." He put out his right hand. Because he seemed to expect it, Rikki shook his hand, still mystified. "I'm David Maxwell."

That didn't clear anything up. "And?" she pressed, feeling as if she were pulling words out of his mouth. Did everyone around here have to be coaxed to talk?

He hooked his thumbs in the belt loops of his jeans, peering into her face. He understood why Beamish had grinned so broadly. "The sheriff didn't tell you about me?"

"I don't know," Rikki said honestly. "Just who are you?"

"I'm the paleontologist from the L.A. Museum. He did tell you he was sending for one, didn't he?"

She nodded. "He said something about an expert." She couldn't help staring. He still looked like a wrangler, more at home on a horse than bending over old bones. "You're a paleontologist?" she couldn't help repeating. Then amusement illuminated her face. "My turn to say I'm sorry. I'm afraid I envisioned a wizened-looking man with glasses."

"I wear contacts. Does that help?"

She felt a little foolish and yet at ease at the same time. She wasn't quite sure how he had managed that. "Won't you come in?" She took a step back from the doorway.

Max hesitated, then looked over his shoulder. He had passed the site of the stable on his way to the house. "If you don't mind, I'd rather get to the site, if it isn't too much trouble."

Rikki pulled the door shut behind her as she shook her head. "No trouble at all. It's right by the house, as you've probably already noticed." She took two steps out onto the porch, then stopped to look up. He was a good foot taller than she was. Maybe more. She shaded her eyes as she looked up at him. The sun was shining brightly directly behind him. "How long have you been a paleontologist?"

"Ten years, according to my degree. In reality, ever since I saw my first dinosaur at the age of five."

Rikki walked with him down the steps. She had always pictured paleontologists as stuffy and methodical. He struck her as too virile, too alive, to be involved in something so... She searched for the right word. The only thing that came to mind was "dead."

Max saw the violet eyes open wide. He had never known anyone with eyes that color. He found himself thinking that they were beautiful. "How long have you been a veterinarian?"

She slid her hands into the back pockets of her jeans as she led the way to the large hole in the ground. "Three years. I've been here for almost a year, but it feels like I just started. The people around here are only just now beginning to accept me," she admitted ruefully, then regretted it. Why was she confiding in a stranger? That wasn't like her.

Max nodded. He knew how leery of outsiders the people in the area could be. "They take their time in giving their seal of approval. But once they do, they stand behind you one hundred percent."

She looked at him in surprise. "You sound like you know them."

"I do. I was born and raised in Senora."

Maxwell. Rikki turned the name over in her head. It wasn't familiar. "Your family move away from here?"

He looked away. "Something like that." They stopped beside the large rectangular hole in the ground. Max looked over the edge. "This it, eh?"

Rikki couldn't help smiling. "I see you're good at your job."

Instead of taking offense, Max flashed an easy, quick grin at her comment. "I'm a fair hand." He squatted down and then slid into the three-foot-deep hole. He turned and offered his hand. "Care to join me?"

She shrugged. "Why not?"

Though she'd intended to slide down on her own, Rikki found herself taking his hand instead. She made the journey a little faster than she had expected, and Max grabbed her by the waist to steady her. Their bodies touched an instant before their eyes did. The moment was frozen in time as they regarded each other with instincts that were almost as old as the fossil that had brought them together.

Rikki cleared her throat self-consciously. "Sorry. Didn't mean to plow into you like that."

He let her go, thinking how small her waist felt. "That's okay," he said lightly. "I needed an afternoon pick-me-up."

Before she could reply, Max had turned his attention to the ground beneath his feet. It gave her a chance to study him in silence. She had always thought that scientists were basically unorthodox, preoccupied people who were somewhat removed from the reality of day-to-day life. This David Maxwell was definitely an exception.

Or was he? From the expression she saw on his face now, he seemed to have suddenly stepped out of the present into a world of his own making. And he wasn't anywhere near the bone.

"The bone is over there." She pointed, but he didn't seem to notice. He was busy turning over rocks and studying them.

Rikki slid her hands back into her pockets and began to move around restlessly. This, she assumed, was going to take some time. Not too much, she hoped. She had work to get back to.

"Look at this!"

Rikki turned around to face him. Max had come out of his mental haze and was excitedly holding up what looked like a common rock to her.

"What is it?" she asked politely.

"Here." Holding it in the palm of his large hand, he traced what looked like faint markings on the underside of the rock. "Can you see?"

"Sure." She squinted. "What am I seeing?"

"A part of a creature that lived millions of years ago."

From the look of glowing enthusiasm on the man's face as he made his pronouncement, Rikki had a sinking feeling that what she was also seeing was a forecast of upheaval in her life as she now knew it.

Chapter Two

The sun was beginning to make her feel uncomfortably hot, Rikki thought as she shifted restlessly. She had tried to remain as polite as possible, staying out of his way and letting him do whatever it was that he was doing. But it was getting to a point where she couldn't stay silent any longer. Her curiosity was steadily getting the better of her. Taking small steps, she slowly approached his squatting form, not wanting to startle him. He didn't even look up. She could have come over with a bulldozer, she realized. He appeared totally engrossed in his work.

"Professor Maxwell," Rikki began tentatively in a low voice.

He was bent over the bone. With long, patient strokes, he was delicately covering it with some sort of thin, translucent coating. After each stroke, he lightly dipped the tip of his small brush into a metal container he had taken out of the pouch he wore slung over his shoulder. "Max," he corrected without bothering to look up.

"Max," she repeated with a slight nod. He looked more like a Max than a professor anyway. "What exactly are you doing?"

Balancing her weight on her heels, she squatted down next to him. The fumes of the mixture he was using became stronger, and she wrinkled her nose.

He turned just then and thought that she looked appealing in her obvious discomfort. He moved the container to the other side, away from her and the drift of the wind. "I'm covering the bone with shellac."

"Why? It seems to have held together for a few hundred thousand years, I'd say, without that."

He laughed at her statement. Rikki wasn't sure if he was patronizing her or not.

"Sixty-five million is more like it, if it's a dinosaur bone, which I believe it is." Tests at the museum would take away any lingering doubt, he thought.

Rikki's mouth dropped open. "Sixty-five—"

"Million," he finished for her. He saw her eyes flicker down to the ground in wonder before they returned to his face. It was the same kind of wonder he always experienced whenever he worked with fossils. He was pleased with her reaction.

"All right." Rikki recovered well. "Sixty-five million, then. Why do you suddenly have to coat it?"

He added one final stroke. "Because, for those sixty-five million years or so, it's been buried, cocooned." He retired the brush. "There, that should hold it until I can have it dug out." Without looking, he screwed the top back on the container. "Now the bone's exposed to the air, and if something isn't done to protect it, it'll decompose rather rapidly. Look." He pointed to three places along one side of the bone and one on the other. "There are several signs that it's already decaying."

Rikki drew a long breath, then let it out. "You learn something every day," she murmured.

Max watched the way the thin white cotton blouse rose and fell over the swell of her breasts as she spoke and told himself that his thoughts weren't very scientific. Pleasurable, but definitely not scientific. "Glad to answer any questions you might have."

Was it her imagination, or had there been something in his eyes just then? She could feel warmth rising to her face and didn't have the vaguest reason why. He hadn't done or said anything to evoke that kind of reaction. At least, not exactly. "All right, answer another one for me."

"If I can."

At least he wasn't the egotistical type, she thought, liking his humility. "This one will be easy, I promise. You've been wandering around here, examining rocks and saying 'hmm,' for at least fifteen minutes. What do all these 'hmms' mean?"

Max smiled broadly but didn't answer her question immediately. He rose, putting the container of shellac and the brush back into his pouch. "They mean that, at least for now, this find appears to be very promising."

He put out his hand, and she took it without thinking, curling her fingers around his. Her eyes met his as she rose to her feet, and she kept her hand where it was a split second longer than necessary. She told herself it was because she was assessing him. He had nice hands, she thought. Capable hands. You could tell a lot about a man by his hands. His were rough from work, yet gentle, despite their size.

Abruptly she pushed her own hands into her back pockets. "Exactly what is it promising?"

Max gestured toward the incline, letting her lead the way back up. He followed close behind. "Fossils, bones, another piece of life's puzzle put in place, or another question raised."

When she faltered in her ascent, he gave her posterior a quick assist. She looked over her shoulder at him, but his face was totally expressionless. She ignored the slight unsettled feeling in the pit of her stomach, calling it juvenile. Her words disguised any trace of her reaction.

"Very philosophical. Could you translate that into layman's language?"

He joined her at the edge of the excavation, then looked back into it as if he hadn't just been down there. "I'd like to conduct a dig here to see what else we can uncover."

"We," she echoed. "How many in a 'we'?"

"Myself. Several other scientists—" He stopped, seeing the reluctance rise in her fascinating eyes. Violet, the color of a warm summer sunset. Absolutely incredible. He discovered that he had to concentrate to regain the focus of the conversation. "Dr. McGuire, do you know what you have here?"

"Trouble," she answered, echoing Roger Whitecastle's initial assessment of the situation.

Max took her arm, leading her back to where his Rover was parked in front of her house. She felt as if she were being buttonholed by a man who was cleverly and quickly spinning a web around her. "No, not trouble, Dr. McGuire—"

"If you're going to hold my arm so tightly and drag me around on my own land, you might as well call me Rikki." She expected him to let go. He didn't. Probably too caught up in his own world to know sarcasm when he hears it, she thought. The only thing that seemed to register was the dismissal of formality.

"Rikki," he said warmly, "this could be an important find."

"All this speculation from one bone and a couple of rocks? How can you tell?"

"I can't," he confessed, "but the signs look good. I won't know if there are any more bones to join the one Roger found until I do some more digging."

So he was on a first name basis with the crusty old man, was he? She had been under the impression that Whitecastle didn't allow anyone but family and trusted friends to call him by his given name. Max was more of an insider than she was. She envied him that.

"You're making me feel that if I say no, I'll be standing in the way of progress, history and Mom's apple pie."

He smiled, nodding. The smile reached his eyes in a way that disarmed her and made her feel the slightest bit uncertain for perhaps the first time in her life. "That's the general idea."

She had to laugh despite herself. "Don't pull any punches, do you?"

"Not when it comes to something like this." His eyes took on an excited haze, turning them almost a smoky gray blue as he went on talking. "Digging into the past, unearthing its secrets, is the most exciting thing in the world."

The past had never held any fascination for her, especially not her own. "I'm afraid the present has always interested me."

He lifted a shoulder, undaunted. The present had always seemed bland to him. "Different opinions are what make the world go round."

He was waiting for her answer. She raised the thick braid from the back of her neck, then let it fall. It was as near a sign of surrender as she would allow herself to give. "Who am I to stand in the way of progress?" She smiled at him. "I guess there's no harm in your looking around, as long as my horses aren't disturbed."

Max's mind was already racing. He could get in contact with Abernathy in San Francisco. He was one of the best geologists around. And Julia was still at the museum. She would know where to round up a crew of eager geology students who could use the grade. She was a top-flight draftswoman, not to mention an excellent photographer. This was going to be good. He could feel it.

By the look in his eyes, Rikki guessed that the man next to her was a million miles away. Make that sixty-five million years away, give or take a million. "Professor Maxwell? Max?"

"Hmm?" He looked at Rikki blankly for a moment, then realized that he had let their conversation evaporate.

Instead of irritating her, his preoccupation amused Rikki. There was a little of the absentminded professor about him after all. "My horses?" she reminded him. "They won't be disturbed?"

He was glad that her cooperation had been won so easily. There was something about this woman, perhaps the way she stood, her weight lightly balanced on the balls of her feet, that told him she could dig in and fight if the spirit moved her. Not that it would do her any good, of course. The law was on his side, but there was no need to rub her nose in that fact. He didn't want to make an opponent of her—for more than one reason, he realized. "You won't even know we're here."

She highly doubted that, but it was a promise she could try to hold him to later if need be.

"Fine. Then we understand each other. When will you be back?" She realized that her question had come out wrong and was afraid that he might reach the wrong conclusion. He was, after all, an attractive man. "To dig, I mean."

He smiled at her quick clarification. "Two days, possibly three." He rubbed his hands together and looked over his shoulder. In his mind, he was already back and at work.

Rikki had seen people look less enthusiastic over winning a high-stakes blackjack game in Las Vegas. For a moment she smiled. She knew what it was like to get caught up in your work or, actually, in your profession. It didn't seem like work when you loved it. More like a way of life. That, more than anything else, had kept her from denying him access to her land. Besides, how long would he stay? Probably just for a little while. It might even prove interesting. Her nephew Elliot was coming for the summer, and this would provide a diversion for him until Max and his crew of scientists left.

"Very well, then." Rikki put out her hand. "I'll see you in a couple of days."

He took her hand, and again that strange, warm feeling filtered through him, a sensation that had nothing to do with old bones and dinosaurs.

"Yes," he said slowly, wondering if he was imagining things, or if she felt it, too, "you will."

The sound of a fast-approaching car splintered the isolated moment until it vanished as if it hadn't happened. Except, Rikki thought, glancing at her hand and still feeling the odd tingle, it had.

"You have visitors," Max observed, climbing into his Land Rover.

"Yes." She shaded her eyes as she looked at the approaching vehicle to verify her suspicions. She smiled. He was early. "My nephew Elliot's coming to spend part of the summer with me."

Max started the car. "Lucky boy."

Rikki glanced back at Max's face, wondering if he was paying her a compliment or if it was just an idle remark. The sexiest smile she had seen in a long time crossed his lips.

No, he definitely didn't fit her image of a scientist, she thought. Elliot might not be the only one who found this situation interesting. The screeching tires brought her attention back to the present.

After fifteen years of driving, Virginia Claremont still drove as if she had just been awarded her license that morning. Her navy blue Mercedes convertible came to an abrupt, teeth-rattling halt just a shade too close to the tan Rover, even though there was a world of space around them.

Rikki braced herself, then let out a sigh as she noted that Virginia had missed becoming intimately bonded to the Rover by an inch—if that much.

"Well, hello," Virginia said brightly, her wide smile directed toward Max rather than Rikki.

Max flashed her a smile and waved his hand at Rikki, then backed up and turned around.

"Who was that?" Virginia asked as she stepped out of the car.

"A paleontologist," Rikki answered, still waiting for her older sister to offer her a greeting. Where attractive men were concerned, everything else seemed to fade for Virginia, even though she was happily married.

Virginia craned her neck in order to watch the departing Rover. "A what?"

"A dinosaur man, Mom," Elliot piped up as he ran out of the car and toward his aunt. "Hi, Aunt Rikki." He threw his arms around her waist and hugged hard.

Rikki smiled and ruffled his brown hair. A warm fondness flooded her veins. She could still remember the day he was born. Virginia had gone into labor so fast that there hadn't been time to get her to the hospital. Rikki had brought Elliot into the world single-handedly. Had that really been nine years ago already? "Hello, Tiger. All ready for the summer?"

"You bet." The enthusiasm on his face was endearing. Much like, she suddenly realized, Max's had been when he was examining the rocks. The two of them would get on well, she decided, pleased with her decision to let the man return.

"What was he doing here?" Virginia looked at Rikki in surprise. "Have you got a beau?"

"No, a bone."

"A what?" Virginia cried, confused.

"I'll explain later."

Rikki glanced over Elliot's head at her sister. That was when she finally saw them. Suitcases. Six of them, piled on top of each other in the back seat. Rikki let her arm drop from Elliot's thin shoulder and took a step forward. "Those are a lot of suitcases for just you, Elliot. Last summer you lived in one pair of jeans and a couple of T-shirts."

Virginia turned around at Rikki's words, but it was Elliot who spoke. "Um, Aunt Rikki, there's been a slight change in plans."

Nine years old and he sounded like a budding lawyer. "How slight?"

Virginia came to stand behind Elliot, her long slender, bejeweled hands on his shoulders as if she were presenting a united front. Or using him as a shield. "I've decided to spend the summer here, Erikka."

Rikki's eyes flashed back to her sister's face. She was hoping to find signs of a poor joke. She failed. "You've what?"

Virginia let just a shred of her dignity falter. Her lower lip trembled a little as she took off her hat and ran her fingers along the brim nervously. "I've decided to spend the summer here," she replied. "I need a vacation, and Wallace is too busy to take one."

Rikki frowned. "Okay, Ginny, out with it, what's going on?"

Virginia grimaced. "Don't call me Ginny. You know how I hate that. It's so—so plebeian-sounding."

"That's always been part of your problem, Virginia," Rikki said, more to herself than to her sister. She leaned against the side of the car and tried again. "All right, whatever your name is, tell me why you're here instead of with Wallace in your nice mansion."

Virginia cast a sidelong glance at her only child. "Not in front of the boy."

The "boy," Rikki firmly believed, had a lot more common sense and intelligence at nine than his mother did at thirty, but she relented. Although she strongly doubted it, there just might be something that wouldn't be good for Elliot to hear.

"Later, then."

The taller woman appeared surprised to win so easily. She allowed a smile to curve her carefully painted lips as she looked inquiringly at her sister. "Then I can stay?"

Sometimes she wondered how Virginia had managed to share a childhood with her and yet learn so little about her. "Virginia, we've had our differences, but I'm not about to throw you out on your ear. If you want to stay here for a while, you can stay." She grinned at her nephew and wrapped her arm around his shoulder again. "After all, you're Elliot's mother." Aunt and nephew laughed, content in the bond that had always been there between them.

Rikki glanced up to see Virginia looking suddenly very left out and alone. She felt a pang, even though she knew the situation went back a long way and was of Virginia's own making. Virginia had modeled herself after their parents.

"C'mon," Rikki offered softly. "I'll help you get settled in."

An anemic smile of thanks creased Virginia's lips; then she looked about apprehensively, as if she'd suddenly remembered something. "Do you still have animals here, Erikka?"

"You mean the horses?" Rikki asked.

Virginia took a deep breath and nodded nervously. "Yes."

Rikki could have sworn her sister's nose went up a fraction of an inch. The only kind of animal Virginia had ever tolerated when they were growing up had been a poodle. A very small, neutered one at that. "Yes, they're still here."

"They can't get loose, can they?" She looked about as if she expected a thundering herd to come racing toward her any second.

"I keep them in a stable, Virginia," Rikki said patiently, wondering if she had just made a colossal mistake, sister or no sister. "Not in a prison."

"I suppose it's all right. Just as long as they don't come near me." Virginia shuddered, then looked around. "Where's your staff?"

"You mean my hired hand?" It amused Rikki that Virginia's view of life was so narrow.

"Yes. What's-his-name, Pedro?"

"Diego," Rikki corrected.

"Him. Where is he?" She indicated the suitcases in the car.

"Visiting his sister in Mexico. She's getting married. He wanted to be there, so I gave him the week off."

To be without hired help was something Virginia couldn't begin to understand. "Then who's going to carry the suitcases?"

"We are," Rikki answered patiently.

A small frown tightened Virginia's lips before she picked up a single article of luggage. It was her makeup case. Without another word, she turned and walked up the stairs, clearly put out.

Rikki exchanged looks with Elliot; then the two of them dug into the back seat. Elliot took his rolled-up sleeping bag and a suitcase that appeared to be his, while Rikki pulled out two of Virginia's suitcases and made her way into the house.

They were opposites, she and Virginia, Rikki thought. Poles apart, right down to their hair. Virginia was a blonde; Rikki was a brunette. Virginia wore her hair short, always in the latest style. Rikki let hers grow, and bound it up carelessly when it got in her way. The former gravitated to the throb of the city; the latter craved the solitude of the country. But the most important difference of all was that Virginia had chosen to model her life on their parents'. Rikki couldn't think of anything that would have made her more unhappy. When they were growing up, it had been Virginia who had danced attendance on their parents' wishes and Rikki who had been lamented over as a black sheep.

And now, Rikki thought, depositing the suitcases on the floor of one of the two spare bedrooms, it was the black sheep who was taking in the golden princess. A dinosaur bone in her backyard and her sister in her house. Who'd've thunk it?

"Will this suit you?" Rikki gestured around the small room. What it lacked in space, it made up for in cheery hominess. At least, she had always thought so. Virginia, from the expression on her face, seemed to have a different opinion.

Virginia looked around, her eyes skimming over the simple light blue wallpaper that had taken Rikki hours to get right. "Is this a bedroom?"

"It has a bed in it, that qualifies it as a bedroom." Rikki told herself not to get annoyed. This arrangement was only temporary. Virginia had probably gotten into an argument with Wallace—undoubtedly of her own creation, if she knew Virginia. But still, Rikki guessed she could afford to be a little forgiving. "Well, now that you know where to put the suitcases," Rikki remarked pointedly, dusting off her hands, "I have work to do. One of my mares is due to foal, and I have to see how she's doing."

"Fold?" Virginia's carefully sculpted eyebrows drew together.

"Foal," Rikki repeated. She linked her fingers together and held them out before her stomach. "With baby horse," she clarified, amused.

Elliot's eyes grew the size of saucers. "Can I come, too?"

Rikki held out her arm, and Elliot fit into the space that was formed. She let her arm drop comfortably around his shoulder. "I was just about to suggest that." Guiding Elliot toward the doorway, Rikki flashed Virginia a smile. "We'll let your mother get accustomed to how the poor folk live."

"You're not poor, Aunt Rikki," Elliot protested as they walked out.

"I never thought so," she agreed.

She heard Virginia muttering something inaudible in the background.

Chapter Three

The sound of a moan penetrated the early-morning air.

Rikki was at a party, surrounded by beautifully dressed, laughing people who kept walking right through her as if she didn't exist. In the midst of all the activity were her parents. She kept trying to get their attention, but each time it appeared that they were turning her way, someone else would pull them aside. The louder she called, the louder the noise at the party grew, drowning her out. And then suddenly she was running between tall buildings, trying desperately to find her way home. Except that she had no idea which way to go and where home was. And still she kept on running, a wall of noise throbbing in her head as she moaned.

Rikki's eyes flew open, her breathing ragged. A dream. It was only a dream. She was safe in her own bed, on her own ranch. Home.

Slowly her breathing steadied.

But if it was only a dream, why hadn't the noise gone away?

She bolted upright, listening. She shook her head, trying to clear it. The noise wasn't fading. It was growing louder.

It was real.

Through bleary eyes, Rikki looked at the digital clock on her nightstand. Six o'clock. Oh Lord, she had overslept, she thought, dragging her hand through her hair. She had meant to get up an hour ago. With Diego gone, there was just too much to do to sleep in like this.

She swung her legs over the side of the bed and sat on the edge. What *was* that noise? It sounded like an automobile, but that was impossible. There was no road running through the middle of her property, at least, not as of last night.

Ignoring the slippers beneath her bed, Rikki padded over to the open bedroom window, pushed the filmy white curtains aside and looked out. An early-morning breeze greeted her face. It was a sensation she usually relished. This morning, she didn't even notice. What she did notice was the activity near her stable site.

Trailers. Four large ones, with another in the distance heading in her direction. And about half a dozen cars, haphazardly parked next to one another in a drunken line around the would-be stable. She didn't recognize any of the vehicles. They didn't belong to anyone in the area. What the devil were they all doing here?

And then the realization suddenly dawned on her semifoggy brain.

Professor David Maxwell. This had to be his doing.

She scanned the area until her eyes fell on him. She saw him approximately one minute before he saw her.

He was conferring with a tall, willowy blonde who looked like someone embarking on an African safari. The woman wore high laced work boots with khaki trousers tucked into the tops, and a white shirt with the sleeves rolled up and rather carelessly unbuttoned at the bust.

Rikki's eyes narrowed. Was that his wife? The stray thought, coming from left field the way it did, startled her. What did she care if he was married? What she cared about, passionately, was that he go about his work quietly, which from where she stood didn't seem possible.

"Max, there's a woman leaning out of the second-story window, looking in our direction and frowning," Julia Teasdale pointed out, using her clipboard as an extension of her arm.

Max turned and glanced toward the house. He knew who it would be without looking. Seeing Rikki, he smiled broadly and beckoned to her, then turned back to continue talking to Julia. "That's the owner."

"She doesn't look very happy," Julia observed. Rikki disappeared from the window. "Uh-oh, I think you're going to be paid a visit shortly." She grinned mischievously. "Did you tell her about Baby?"

Max looked toward the bulldozer that was just now rumbling into position at the outer perimeter of the stable's unfinished foundation. He had requested that it be brought "just in case." That wasn't going to make Rikki's accepting it any easier, he suspected. "No, I didn't really get a chance to bring it up."

"I think," Julia said as Rikki appeared in the distance, walking toward him determinedly, "you're going to get your chance now." She tapped his shoulder with her clipboard. "Lots of luck, Max. I've got to see to the students."

"Coward."

"That's me, through and through."

Max had no time to watch Julia walk off toward the geology students whom she had rounded up after he called her late Thursday evening. His thoughts went to Rikki. He had a feeling he had a few ruffled feathers to smooth.

Rikki was wearing her long blue robe loosely sashed at her waist. The gusting breeze playfully teased open the sides as she approached him, treating Max to the sight of long, well-shaped legs that were just barely covered by the oversize T-shirt she wore beneath it. She was barefoot, too.

For a moment Max allowed the business at hand to slip into second place as he looked appreciatively at the image Rikki projected. Pure, smoldering womanhood. He felt something very basic, very male, within him being drawn to her. It occurred to him that he hadn't realized earlier that she was quite this attractive. With sleep-tousled hair and a delinquent robe playing hide-and-seek with her legs, she made quite an unconsciously, seductively inviting picture. He wasn't the only one who was noticing. He heard several male voices commenting in the background.

Max drew a deep breath, reminding himself that he wasn't here to stare at a perfect specimen of womanhood but to unearth a leftover specimen from the era when dinosaurs moved freely about, unencumbered by deliciously sexy-looking women who looked as if they had an ax to grind.

In her bare feet, Rikki hardly reached his shoulder. It didn't stop her from seeming like an opponent to be wary of. "Professor Maxwell," she announced formally, "I have a bone to pick with you."

"Not any of the ones in the ground, I hope." As he spoke, he nodded toward the second trailer. His. "Care for a cup of coffee?"

She was annoyed at the way he had deceived her, and now he was trying to placate her with coffee! The man was impossible! She gave a sharp shake of her head. "I didn't come here for coffee, Professor Maxwell."

"Max," he reminded her soothingly, casually taking her elbow and moving her toward his trailer anyway. There was a small table set up in front of it with an automatic coffeemaker. "I realize that. You probably make better coffee than I do." He poured one steaming mug and then another. "Still, I thought that making a hospitable offer might quell the fire in your eyes." He glanced at her casually over his shoulder. "Do you know you have fascinating eyes?"

Oh no, he wasn't going to get around her with flattery, no matter how appealingly rugged he looked in his work shirt and jeans. "And they have twenty-twenty vision."

"Better than mine." He lifted a jar of nondairy creamer. "Cream?"

"No. Max!" she fairly shouted to make him pay attention.

"Yes?" he asked calmly, his dark gray-blue eyes looking into hers.

She was aware of something going on beneath the surface, but she just couldn't put her finger on it. With an effort, she pushed it away. "When I gave you permission to conduct a—" She stopped, hunting for the word.

"Dig?" he supplied amiably.

"Dig," she repeated, "I didn't mean for you to move a mini-city onto my property."

He turned and looked over his shoulder, with one sweeping glance taking in the people he had led onto her land. There were fifteen in all. Not a small number, but not exactly a city, either. He looked down into her annoyed, upturned face and wondered what it would feel like to kiss away her frown. It was a surprising thought, and it disturbed him. "You won't even know we're here, I promise."

How could he say such a thing? Did he think she was feebleminded?

"Unless I was struck deaf at six o'clock this morning, there would be no way I wouldn't know you were here," she cried, gesturing. She stopped, seeing the bulldozer for the first time. Her eyes widened. "And what is *that?*"

He looked in the direction she was waving, although he really didn't need to. Julia was right. He should have mentioned Baby to Rikki sooner. "It's a bulldozer."

"I know what it is." She gritted her teeth together, searching for strength. "What I want to know is, what's it doing on my property?"

"Sitting, at the moment." He pressed a coffee mug into her hands and then gave her an apologetic smile that unsettled the pit of her stomach, despite her annoyance. "Sorry, poor attempt at humor. Why don't you have some of this? It might make you feel better."

Nothing was going to make her feel better. Her life was very obviously being disrupted on all sides. But his apology did take some of the edge off her temper.

"What is it doing here?" she repeated more calmly, taking the cup. "And what are all these people doing here?"

"They're here to work the dig," Max informed her simply. He was having trouble keeping his eyes on her face. The top of her robe was separating with each gesture she made, and the neck of her T-shirt was slipping, offering a view that made him firmly believe that not all bones were created equal.

"All of them?" Rikki noticed the amused glimmer in his eyes when he glanced at her, and she looked down. With a regal movement she put down the mug and drew her robe together, this time firmly knotting the sash at her waist.

She had a small waist, he noted, just made for a man's hands. He felt his own hands itch slightly. Forcing his mind back to the topic, he lifted the mug she had put down and offered it to her again.

Rikki took it without being aware of her action. Her mind was on the people milling around. "I thought you'd bring back a few other paleontologists and you'd work the ground with small picks and whisk brooms."

He saw her slight flush and didn't want her to feel foolish. "That's part of it, too," he assured her.

She felt as if he were patronizing her. "A bulldozer hardly falls into the same category as whisk brooms."

"Baby's just here in case we need to move a lot of earth."

"Baby?"

He grinned at the look of confusion on her face. "An affectionate name one of my students once gave the bulldozer."

Her curiosity about this man seemed to be a given, even with all this going on. She moved the mug in her hands, feeling the warmth, telling herself that was the only source of warmth she was experiencing, telling herself that she hadn't undergone just the smallest flush of pleasure when he had looked at her that way, making her feel like a woman first, last and always. "Students? You were a teacher?"

"Only for a year, but I was referring to one of the workers. We usually use students."

"Cheap labor?" she asked, raising one eyebrow.

"Can't get any cheaper than free," he laughed, agreeing. "It also gives them firsthand experience, which is invaluable."

She didn't know about that. Retreating for a moment to collect her thoughts and remove herself from the effect of his smile, Rikki contemplated the effect his work was going to have on her life as she took a long sip of her coffee.

She felt as if she were swallowing sludge. "Strong," she mumbled, her eyes watering.

"Wakes you up."

She handed the mug back to him. "More like stands you on your ear."

"Don't tell me you don't like my coffee."

"All right, I won't."

Rikki looked toward the long hole in the ground and frowned as she saw two students pitching a tent right over the area containing the protruding bone.

They were settling in. She wasn't happy about this, but she had given her permission and was loath to renege. Something about a person's word being their bond nagged at her conscience.

"I'll be happy to sample yours someday."

His words brought her attention back to him. He was looking down into her face, and was so close that her heart leapt into her throat.

Silly expression, she thought. Her heart was where it had always been—just beating a little harder, that was all. And that was probably because she had just consumed a ton of caffeine in that one sip of the brew he had mislabeled coffee.

"Excuse me?"

"Your coffee. I'd be happy to sample it someday. Purely for scientific reasons, of course. To make a comparison test."

She liked the way amusement danced in his eyes, even though his expression remained serious. "You sound more like a comparison shopper than a paleontologist."

"I believe in leaving myself open to everything."

He was being so amiable that she felt a little like the wicked witch swooping down on him. Still, the idea of a bulldozer tearing up the land, her land, looking for something she had absolutely no interest in, destroying her peace and quiet, did not sit well with her.

Max saw her look toward the bulldozer as if it were an adversary. "We won't use it unless we absolutely have to, Rikki."

The way he said her name made it sound almost like a caress. "Famous last words," she muttered.

He crossed his heart and raised his right hand. "And I promise to let you know beforehand."

"And then I'll have six and a half minutes to clear out the horses," she said dryly. Suddenly, her eyes opened wide, and she turned on her heel and hurried away from him.

Surprised, Max followed her. Out of the corner of his eye, he saw Julia watching them. She raised her shoulders and then let them drop, indicating her confusion. He shook his head. He had no idea what had made Rikki leave him like that.

But he was going to find out.

She went straight to the stable. The agitation within the small wooden building was easy to pick up as soon as she entered. Rikki's attention was all for the horse in the farthest stall.

"It's all right, Sugar," she whispered soothingly, running her hand along the palomino's white-starred muzzle. "Just a little noise, that's all." Rikki sensed Max walking in behind her. She looked over her shoulder. "This," she said accusingly, "was what I was afraid of. All this commotion is scaring them."

Max joined her on the other side of the mare. "It's new." He looked the mare over. "They'll settle down." With soft, easy movements, he stroked the horse's neck. "How soon is she due?"

Rikki watched his hand move as if she were hypnotized by it. So strong, yet so gentle. What would that hand feel like . . .

She drew her eyes up to his face, banishing the question from her thoughts. She felt as if he could read her mind, but there wasn't a triumphant look on his face. He wasn't an easy man to figure out. His hand brushed up against hers. Rikki drew her hand away. "She's due very soon, so I don't want her upset."

"We're not going to upset you, beauty," Max said to the horse. "You'll get used to us, won't you, girl?"

To Rikki's surprise, the mare seemed to calm a bit, responding to Max's gentle voice and touch. "Are you trying to charm her?"

"Doing my very best."

Did all paleontologists have mischievous eyes? She didn't know, but this one certainly did. "You seem to be succeeding." She folded her arms in front of her. It seemed the robe was trying to work its way loose again.

Satisfied that the horses were all right, at least for the time being, Rikki led the way out of the stable. "I'm going to have to think about this, Max." She began to push the door closed.

Max completed the action for her, then watched as she locked it. "I understand your concern, Rikki, but I don't mean your horses any harm."

She glanced at her watch. Six-thirty, and she still wasn't dressed. The last time that had happened, she'd been in high school. Already he was throwing things off kilter for her. She began to walk hurriedly toward the house. Max stretched his legs to keep up.

"Sugar lost her last foal. I don't want to see that happen again."

"Neither do I."

Rikki looked up at his face. There wasn't a hint of a smile. "I believe you mean that."

"I do. But I also don't want to lose the chance of finding another link to the past."

They reached the front porch. Rikki took two steps and turned, her face level with his. "When I lived in L.A. I saw literature on dinosaurs everywhere. Does the world really need another dinosaur?"

"Yes. And so do I."

She knew he meant it. He had a need—she sensed it. A need like her own, to give a purpose to his life. Hers was working with living animals. His was uncovering prehistoric ones.

She turned and walked into the house. This time, he followed her in. "You never know," he told her, trailing her into the kitchen, "what the next discovery might yield. The missing link might be under your property."

Rikki stopped and turned to see if he was serious. He was smiling again, but it was a semiserious smile. Maybe he *was* serious, at that. "Or the abominable snow-man," she cracked.

"Maybe. And you're standing in the way of all that information." He leaned a hip against the kitchen counter, his face inches away from hers. Her eyes met his, and a warm rush of air swirled around her. Suddenly the atmosphere crackled with tension that had very little to do with horses and dinosaurs.

Rikki looked away.

Max took a moment to regain his bearings. She had eyes that made him forget everything except his name. When his pulse steadied, his mind began working rapidly. He wasn't going to let this discussion end unfavorably. It couldn't. Yet he was still reluctant to use strong-arm tactics to get his way. Things could easily be settled by telling her that she had no rights to the minerals on her land. The county retained those, and in so doing, they gave him the right to conduct excavations on her property if something benefiting the public could be discovered. But he didn't want to tell her that, didn't want to bring in the sheriff to tell her. He wanted to coax her, to cajole her, into giving her consent. He wanted, he knew, to make her see things his way. Through his eyes.

"Please, Rikki." Without thinking, he touched her arm, forcing her to look at him. "Don't tell me you've decided to reconsider."

He never liked to use pressure, but he was especially averse to using it with Rikki. He didn't want to give her cause to dislike him. There was something about young Dr. McGuire that cut through his self-contained, work-related world and spoke to his inner being. He wanted to be her friend. And maybe more. He had felt it as soon as he met her. It startled him a little, and perhaps even worried him. He hadn't felt that way since Sally, and that had ended disastrously.

Rikki sighed impatiently and took another look at Max's face. There was sincerity written all over it. It reminded her of a puppy. She'd always been a sucker for puppies. Rikki made her decision.

"Maybe I can get Mr. Whitecastle to work a little faster so I can move the horses to another area."

Max began to thank her, but Virginia picked that moment to walk in. Wearing an emerald silk dressing gown that floated behind her as she made her entrance, she looked far from happy.

"What is all this commotion?" she demanded, holding her head. It was obvious that she didn't see Max as she walked in. "Do you have any idea what time it is? I thought you ran away to the country to get some solitude. There's less noise on the 405 freeway during rush hour. Oh!" She blinked, coming to a halt before Max.

"Morning, ma'am," he said politely. Rikki thought his voice had taken on more of a lazy drawl than it had had a moment ago.

Virginia spared one accusing glance for Rikki before she turned her eyes back to Max. "Erikka, why didn't you tell me you had a guest?" Her hand automatically flew to her hair. "I must look a sight."

Max knew by the way she fluttered her eyes what the woman was hunting for. It cost him nothing to supply it. "For sore eyes," he assured her.

"Is he saying that you make his eyes sore, Mom?" Elliot asked, stumbling in behind her as he rubbed the sleep from his own.

"Hush, Elliot, don't interrupt Mr.—" Virginia looked from Max to Rikki for help.

"Professor David Maxwell, this is my sister Vir—"

"—ginia Claremont," Virginia completed, putting her hand into Max's. She smiled up at him warmly. It was obvious to Max by the way she looked at him that she was sizing him up. "You must be the paleontologist that Erikka's been raving about."

Rikki stared at her sister, her mouth falling open as Max turned back toward her and grinned.

Chapter Four

When the smile rose to Max's lips, Rikki amended her initial assessment of his appearance. The sincere, innocent puppy-dog countenance had been transformed into a sexy, warm, inviting expression. Were puppy dogs sexy? she wondered. Maybe. To other puppy dogs.

Rikki realized that her thoughts were scattering, making little sense. A sure sign that she was embarrassed. Leave it to Virginia to reduce her to the shy, awkward girl she had once been, standing before her father, complete with falling socks, enduring perpetual parental disapproval because she continually failed to measure up.

Except that this time Virginia was doing it in Rikki's home territory, where she had some control. Rikki leveled an irritated look at her sister as she pulled her sash even tighter around her waist. "I think the word 'raving' is stretching it, Ginny."

Max glanced from one woman to the other. "I'm sure if you were raving, Rikki, it wasn't about me, it was *because* of me."

He saw Rikki's expression relax and knew he had hit a responsive chord. Admittedly he wasn't terribly good in awkward social situations, but he knew trouble when he saw it. He anticipated plenty of problems in the weeks ahead if this dig proved as fruitful as he hoped it would. There was no reason to alienate Rikki at the outset, or make her feel uncomfortable around him because of a thoughtless remark.

He leaned his hip against the counter as he studied Virginia unobtrusively. Rikki's sister didn't look anything like her. Their personalities, based on the little he'd witnessed, were totally diverse, as well. Virginia tossed her sentences around carelessly. The word "shallow" came to mind, and he felt a touch of pity for the blonde. Whereas Rikki made him think of a woman of substance. Actually, Rikki made him think, period.

It was time to harness his thoughts. They were beginning to flow along unknown, unfamiliar avenues.

"Now, if you don't mind . . ." Max began to make his way to the back door. Experience had taught him that it was best to leave on a positive note.

But his path was blocked by a gangly boy who appeared to be all elbows, bony shoulders and knobby knees beneath beige-and-brown-striped pajamas. There was an incredibly hopeful expression across every inch of his face that Max couldn't possibly ignore. Rikki had mentioned a nephew. This had to be him.

"Are you really looking for a dinosaur here?" Elliot asked.

Rikki was amazed at the wonder she heard in Elliot's voice. She knew he liked dinosaurs. What kid between the ages of five and fifteen didn't, these days? But she had never seen him talk to a stranger without being prodded first. Obviously the prospect of dinosaurs had a way of cutting through Elliot's natural shyness. Maybe having that fossil turn up would be good for something after all. She'd been desperate to find a way to help Elliot get out of his shell.

"As hard as I can," Max answered.

Since the boy wasn't moving, Max carefully went around him, still trying to gain access to the door. With public relations smoothed over for the time being, he was anxious to get to work. A new dig always excited him.

Elliot looked toward Rikki, a silent question in his eyes. Rikki nodded her encouragement. Elliot chewed on his lower lip for a moment longer, debating. He took another step forward, once again getting in Max's way. "Can I, um, maybe, um..." He looked afraid of finishing, afraid of being rejected.

Virginia swooped over to her son. "Elliot, you don't want to get in this nice man's way, now," she chided, her eyes on Max. A beautifully manicured hand reached out from beneath the silk kimono sleeve to grasp the boy's shoulder.

Max wondered how she managed to get dressed in the morning with nails that looked as if they were a good inch and a half long.

"But I'm not going to get in—" Elliot began to protest.

Virginia's hold on her son's shoulder became a little firmer. "Yes, you are."

The light went out of Elliot's eyes. That was all that Rikki needed. "Would you mind very much if he watched?'' she asked Max, purposely avoiding Virginia's face and the reprimanding look she knew was there.

"Well, I, um . . ."

Although he found something very appealing about the way Rikki rose up like a lioness coming to her cub's rescue, Max didn't really want to have anyone around the dig who wasn't essential to the work being done. The last thing he needed right now was a little boy bombarding him with a lot of meaningless questions, distracting him and getting in his way.

Rikki didn't want to ask Max for any favors. But after all, she was letting him tear up part of her property. The least he could do was accommodate one small boy. "Elliot's very keen on dinosaurs."

Elliot moved his shoulder, shrugging off his mother's grasp. Virginia's expression reflected her surprise. Elliot ignored her as he interjected excitedly, "Aunt Rikki bought me a whole set of books on them last Christmas."

Max felt hemmed in. He looked from the boy to Rikki. The look in her eyes told him that this boy was very special to her. If he said no, that element of discomfort he was trying to diplomatically avoid would meet him head-on. And he found himself having just the slightest bit of difficulty saying no to eyes the color of African violets. Besides, the look on Elliot's face brought back the memory of another gangly boy who felt he didn't quite fit in, either, until he found his own world. A world filled with dinosaurs.

Max lifted his broad shoulders and let them drop casually. "Sure, we can always use another pair of hands." The wide grin on Elliot's face was worth whatever problems might arise because of his presence. When

Max looked up and saw Rikki's expression of approval, it reinforced his feelings. "And now, if you'll—"

"Will you be here for dinner?"

Max was beginning to feel that finishing a sentence was not an easy matter in this household. He was going to have to learn to talk faster. Now it was Virginia who was blocking the exit.

Rikki spoke slowly, emphasizing each word. "Virginia, I'm sure that Max has made his own dinner arrangements." She wasn't about to have him browbeaten into eating with them just because Virginia was on another one of her social-butterfly kicks.

"Well, actually—" Max began, uncertain about the expression on Rikki's face. He hadn't really thought about dinner. His thoughts hadn't gotten that far into the day. Julia always took care of making sure the crew was provided for. Seeing to food wasn't his department. He was too busy supervising everything involved with unearthing traces of a life that had existed millions of years ago. Food, the present and anything unrelated to the dig had a way of fogging up for him.

Rikki read the mild confusion in his face. Was it just Virginia, or something simpler? "You haven't made arrangements for food?" Rikki hazarded. The slight, endearing flush that passed quickly over his face told her she had guessed correctly.

He didn't want to seem like the epitome of an absentminded professor. That was what Sally had called him when she had unceremoniously dumped him for "someone with a future, not a dull past." Even now, after ten years, the words, if not the memory, stung. He glanced over his shoulder, as if that would make Julia materialize in the room. "One of the others takes care of that kind of detail for—"

It was all Virginia needed to hear. "It's settled, then. You'll be here for dinner." Virginia stroked the collar of her kimono, obviously certain that the battle had been won.

Rikki didn't want Max to feel obligated to eat with them. If she didn't do something, Virginia was going to steamroll over both of them. She had to put a stop to this. For a second she forgot about Max as she turned toward her sister. "Maybe Professor Maxwell doesn't want to eat here."

"Oh, but I do."

The words seemed to come out on their own, surprising two of them, completely pleasing the third.

Virginia laced her long fingers together and smiled at her sister. "I think I'll go up to my room now and get dressed."

If her self-satisfied smile had been wider, her eyes would have disappeared altogether, Rikki thought.

Virginia turned, fully aware of having an audience, and slowly made her exit.

Rikki cleared her throat. It was a nervous gesture, and she hated it, but it came of its own volition. She gathered her composure and turned toward Max, catching him by surprise. He was studying her, *all* of her. Again she felt embarrassed—but pleased.

Had he just been polite, or did he really want to come to dinner? Life was getting complicated again. She had thought she had left complications behind by moving out here. Obviously not.

"Well, dinner will be at six-thirty, if that's all right with you." She had no idea why she'd asked that. She wasn't about to change the time for him. Dinner was going to be served at the same time it was always served. Virginia's casual invitation to Max had thrown her off.

Served her right for being softhearted and letting Ginny stay. She should have sent her back to Wallace to iron out whatever it was that needed ironing. Shorthanded, with a dinosaur bone turning up in her backyard, Rikki didn't need Virginia adding to the turmoil.

"That'll be fine with me."

Rikki looked at him blankly for a minute, forgetting what it was that he was agreeing to.

"Dinner," Max prompted, when he saw her expression. "Six-thirty." He knew that look well. It was pre-occupation. He'd been guilty of it himself more times than he cared to remember. Although Sally had been quick to point it out to him often enough.

Damn, why was he thinking of Sally after all this time? Granted, this was where it had all begun. And ended. All within the confines of Senora. A love affair that was supposed to last forever, but didn't. In part, that was why he had left, to forget and to start over. And to find his rainbow's end. Or his dinosaur, he amended. But it was more than ten years in the past. Too insignificant for him to dwell on when he could well be on the brink of something big.

"Fine," Rikki murmured. She went to shove her hands into her back pockets and realized that she was still standing around in her robe. She swallowed an oath. Everything was off schedule this morning.

"I can change and be down in five minutes," Elliot promised, coming to life and backing away toward the stairs. He bumped into a chair.

"You can brush your teeth and be back in ten," Rikki instructed affectionately. She watched as Elliot steadied the chair. "And don't forget your glasses." She knew how much he hated wearing them, but seeing took precedent over discomfort.

A frown played on Elliot's face as he looked down at the kitchen floor. His glasses were what he disliked most about himself. They were his cross to bear, another thing that singled him out and gave the other kids something to tease him about.

Max was quick to pick up the signs. "I wear contacts myself."

Elliot's head jerked up, and then a grateful smile flittered across his face. "I will, too, when I'm older," he confided, then quickly dashed toward the back stairs.

So you can empathize. Nice to know. Rikki turned her attention back to Max. "Thank you."

He liked the way her smile crinkled the corners of her eyes. There seemed to be a whole list of things he liked about her. It wasn't like him to get carried away like this. "For what?"

She nodded toward the disappearing boy. "For saying that." Rikki settled for burrowing her hands in the shallow pockets of her robe. "Elliot's very self-conscious about the things that make him stand out." Her voice softened, fondness seeping in the way it always did when she spoke about her nephew. "He's taller than the rest, thinner, and smarter." She emphasized the last with pride. "He hasn't learned yet that marching to a different drummer can be a good thing."

He could have used an Aunt Rikki when he was growing up, Max mused. "And you have?"

"Yes, I have," she told him.

The ranch she owned was like so many of the others in the area. He didn't quite see the point she was making. "Doesn't seem so different to me." He leaned his elbow on the counter, his face lowering to hers.

He was a little too close for comfort, although she wasn't quite sure why she was uncomfortable. It wasn't that he represented any sort of threat, except perhaps to her peace of mind. It was just that he was there. She edged away a step. "That's because you don't know my background. Trust me, this is different."

Max straightened, wondering what had prompted her to move back. "Maybe you can tell me over dinner."

She thought of Virginia. "Virginia will undoubtedly monopolize the conversation." Besides, she didn't like sharing her feelings with Virginia around. Her older sister had never understood what motivated her, and Rikki had long since given up trying to make her understand. "Maybe some other time."

The lady's private life was off-limits. Well, why not? Wasn't that the way he felt about his? He shrugged, perhaps a little too casually. "Whatever." He turned to walk out.

"Aren't you forgetting something?"

He looked at her, confused. He hadn't come in with anything. "What?"

"Your assistant." Rikki nodded toward the back stairs. She watched how his eyes followed hers. There was just the slightest look of apprehension there. "Don't worry, Elliot will stay out of your way unless you ask him to help." In case he was going to take Elliot's absence as an opportunity to beg off, she hurriedly added, "I've never seen him this excited before, except when he's around the horses. He tends to keep to himself a lot."

Max could relate to that. Solitude had proven to be his best friend, until he had met Allen and found someone who shared his passion for dinosaurs. But then, Allen did everything with a passion. "He seems comfortable with you."

"That's because I adore him." Rikki laughed, and he found that he liked the sound. There was something fresh and infectious about it. In fact, there was something fresh and infectious about *her.*

The knock on the back door startled them both. Rikki turned and saw the woman in the safari outfit holding up a clipboard and gesturing toward Max through the back window. Rikki pulled open the door, which squeaked in protest. She had to remember to oil the hinges when she got a chance. Maybe sometime within the next year, she thought with an inward sigh.

"Hi, I'm Julia Teasdale." Julia took Rikki's hand and shook it, looking a good deal fresher than Rikki felt at that moment. "I tried knocking on the front door, but no one heard." Julia didn't wait to be invited in.

"Small wonder, with all this noise," Rikki murmured as she closed the back door again.

"Max." Julia sailed past Rikki, the clipboard an extension of her hand. "I wanted you to take a look at the work shifts."

"Shifts?" Rikki echoed as she joined them.

"We thought we'd get the maximum use of all this daylight. The faster we work, the faster we're out of here." So it was a little white lie, but there was no harm in it, he thought, taking the proffered clipboard. He purposely avoided Rikki's eyes.

"The faster you work, the noisier you work," Rikki pointed out. She still hadn't reconciled herself to the bulldozer. If it was there, it was there for a reason. She had a feeling Max was only trying to soften the initial blow. Nobody dragged around a bulldozer purely on a whim.

Max was busy flipping through the sheets of paper Julia had compiled before arriving in Senora. The woman was nothing if not thorough, he thought in admiration. "Not necessarily," he told Rikki in response to her comment. He handed the clipboard back to Julia. "Looks fine to me."

By the expression on Julia's face, Rikki surmised that the woman had expected him to be satisfied. She wondered how long they had worked together. And if work was all there was between them.

None of your business if it isn't, she reminded herself.

She became alert as Max fell into step behind the departing woman. He was leaving without Elliot, and she was afraid that the boy would take that as a sign that he really wasn't wanted around the site. She began to call him back when another voice beat her to it.

"Professor?"

Max looked over toward the source of the small, uncertain childish voice. He smiled more to himself than to Elliot. He had forgotten all about the boy. Someday he was going to do something about his memory. Max put out his hand toward Elliot, beckoning him forward.

"You're just in time to accompany me to the site." He placed a tentative hand on Elliot's shoulder. "Julia, this is our new assistant, Elliot."

Julia flashed Elliot a warm smile that had Rikki reassessing the woman's virtues. "Pleased to meet you, Elliot."

Elliot stopped abruptly, just short of the door. He looked at Rikki sheepishly over his shoulder, pushing his glasses back up his nose. "Aunt Rikki, I'll help you with the horses later."

She would have been hard-pressed to think of another nine-year-old who was so conscientious. Rikki grinned and waved him off. "Don't give it another thought."

And, from the look of rapture on his face as he trotted out between Max and Julia, Rikki was certain that Elliot wouldn't.

Alone in the kitchen, Rikki looked at her watch, then sucked in her breath. It was almost seven. There were chores piling up by the second. She decided to postpone her shower until later and just throw on a T-shirt and jeans for now.

Hurrying up the stairs, she glanced toward Virginia's room. It would have been nice to have some help with the work. But with Elliot elevated to the level of "assistant," there was no one left. Diego wasn't due back for another three days, and the idea of asking Virginia was out of the question. Virginia probably didn't know which end of a pitchfork to use, anyway. A sudden image of her sister standing in the stable, mucking out a stall, brought a smile to Rikki's lips.

She was about to walk into her room to get dressed, then changed her mind. Virginia's cavalier invitation to Max replayed itself in her head. Time was precious if she was to get everything done by dinner, but Rikki couldn't afford to let things get out of hand so soon into Virginia's visit. There was no telling what her sister, left unbridled, was capable of.

Taking a deep breath, she knocked once on Virginia's door. There was no answer, but she hadn't really expected one. When she pushed the door open, she found Virginia lying in bed.

Virginia bolted upright, surprised at the intrusion. Surprise gave way to annoyance. "I could have been getting dressed."

Rikki shook her head, not about to be intimidated. Virginia was using her "errant servant" voice. "Not at this hour. Don't forget, I know you. Given half a chance, you'd sleep until noon." Rikki crossed her arms before her, resting her shoulder against the doorjamb. "Besides, you haven't got anything I haven't seen before."

Virginia's eyes narrowed. "Doesn't the word 'privacy' mean anything to you?"

Rikki straightened, her expression growing serious. "Yes, it does, but I was beginning to think that it didn't to you."

Virginia lay back against her pillows, squirming a little to get comfortable. She frowned at Rikki. "What *are* you talking about?"

She might have known that Virginia wouldn't understand. "Your invitation to Max."

"Oh." Virginia smiled, looking down at her nails. "That went rather well, I thought."

Maybe a two-by-four, applied across her thick skull, would help. "Virginia, this is my house."

Virginia wrinkled her nose, looking up. "Well, of course it is. This certainly isn't a place that I would live in voluntarily."

Rikki thought about telling her sister to pack up and leave, but she bit the words back. Virginia probably didn't realize she'd just insulted her. The woman never thought out the full implication of her words.

Rikki tried another approach. "The point is that I get to decide who comes to dinner, not you."

Virginia looked at her, puzzled. "Don't you want him to come?"

"Yes, but—"

Virginia flashed a smile that was at once innocent and patronizing. "Then what's the problem?"

Rikki sighed. It was like trying to thread a needle with a rock. "Years of broken-down communications, I suspect." She began to leave, but Virginia's next words brought her to a full stop.

"Erikka, I think you've lived by yourself much too long. You're just not making any sense. I'm glad I was here for you."

Rikki looked at her sister sharply. "Virginia, just what do you have in mind?"

Virginia smoothed out the bedclothes. "You need a man," she said without bothering to look up. If she had, she would have seen the darkening clouds gathering in Rikki's eyes.

Virginia could be absolutely infuriating at times. *Most* times. Rikki recalled hearing almost the exact same words coming out of her mother's mouth. Only then they had sounded haughtier. "This is not the nineteenth century, Virginia. I do *not* need a man to be a complete person."

This time Virginia did look up. There had been something almost dangerous in Rikki's voice. "Then why are you so irritable?"

Rikki opened her mouth to answer, then told herself to cool off first. Only hurt feelings would result if she answered now, and besides, Virginia wouldn't understand. She never did. She was too much her parents' daughter to see that there could be a different way of life, a fulfilling way of life even if you weren't Mrs. So-and-so. *Especially* if you weren't Mrs. So-and-so, Rikki amended. Marriage hadn't, apparently, brought Virginia everlasting happiness, even though Wallace Claremont was a basically decent sort of man, if you liked stuffed shirts.

"I have stables to clean." Rikki turned on her heel and marched out.

"Ugh, that would make me irritable, too." Virginia's voice followed Rikki as she went to her own room to change.

She shut the door a little bit too hard. "Slammed" was more like it, she thought. A feeling of release followed. Rikki didn't believe in letting things fester. There was no point.

There was no point, Rikki repeated to herself as she led Buttercup into the makeshift corral before cleaning out her stall, in getting worked up about Virginia. She would just roll with the punches, the way she had when they were growing up. She certainly knew what her older sister was like. Time hadn't changed the fact that Virginia was incapable of an original thought, lived her life the way her parents had before her and existed only to attend one social function after another.

Still, Rikki mused, Virginia was here for some reason. Perhaps paradise wasn't as satisfying as Virginia always claimed it was.

Rikki frowned, removing Buttercup's halter. Instead of snapping at her sister, maybe she should ask her a few questions to see just what had happened to prompt Virginia to want to stay out here. The ranch had certainly never been on the list of her favorite places.

The mare nudged her as Rikki stood, thinking. "Sorry, Buttercup. I'm letting my mind wander, and this isn't the day for that." She stroked the velvet muzzle lovingly. The din in the background, coming from people shouting to one another, made Rikki wince. "How are you holding up with all this, girl?"

The horse snorted, making Rikki laugh. "Yeah, me too. It won't be long. They'll be here for a week or so, and then, when they don't come up with anything else, they'll be gone. I promise."

Rikki looked over toward the site and saw that Max had stopped whatever he'd been doing and was just standing there, watching her. She waved, then dropped her hand. The idea of Max and crew leaving made her feel inexplicably sad. She wondered why. It didn't make any sense. That was what she wanted, wasn't it? To have peace and quiet restored again. Maybe, as Virginia had so ineloquently pointed out, she *was* alone too much.

Rikki turned and went to clean the stables before any more time slipped away from her. She had no time for such ridiculous thoughts.

Chapter Five

Where his work was concerned, Max had been accused of having tunnel vision, of blocking out the living. That was the reason, he mused, that he hadn't been able to sustain the one long-term relationship he had attempted in his life. He found things from the distant past far more compelling than things in the present.

Well, he wasn't preoccupied by the past now. The work was there, yet he wasn't immersed in it to the exclusion of everything and everyone else.

The fault didn't lie with the boy, who was eager to help, eager to learn, who, once encouraged, had an endless stream of quite intelligent questions to ask. He could readily have assimilated the boy's presence into the scheme of things. Max had worked with eager students before; he had been one himself once. Having people around asking questions went with the territory. No, he couldn't blame this odd feeling, his distraction, on Elliot. The source was elsewhere.

Max tried to shut out the distraction, but it kept slipping through his barriers, infiltrating his thoughts at the oddest moments, catching him unaware. Somehow *she* kept floating into his mind. Walking toward him in her robe, the breeze playing with the edges, devilishly teasing him with a view first of her calf, then her thigh. Teasing him with what it *wasn't* showing him. What was there just beneath, for him to see and maybe sample.

The only fantasies Max had ever entertained had all concerned dinosaurs and the discovery thereof. Even when he had thought he was in love with Sally, there had been a barrier in his mind beyond which thoughts of her did not penetrate. Work was very important to him; it always had been. Sally had been very important to him, too. But she hadn't wanted to be of equal importance; she had wanted to come first, and he hadn't been able to manage that, not for long. He *needed* to work, to be involved in unearthing the secrets of a world others could only imagine. He had told her that, and his honesty had cost him his fiancée. But Max had never developed the fine art of deceit. That was for others to ply.

He considered himself a mild-mannered, even-tempered man. His fantasies reflected his temperament. That had seemed normal to him. The thoughts he was having now were totally out of character.

And he hardly knew her, he thought as he watched Rikki lead yet another horse into the rope corral. What kind of thoughts was he going to have about her after a few weeks? And how would they affect his work?

"How come you're stopping?"

Elliot's question broke through his momentary trance. Max looked down at the boy by his side. "What?" A stray glance in Julia's direction told him that she had noted his odd behavior, as well.

"You're not working." Elliot nodded at the small fragment of bone he had stopped shellacking. "You're looking at Aunt Rikki."

"Oh." The boy seemed to notice everything, Max thought. "I was just wondering." He turned his attention back to the fragment on the makeshift worktable before him. Dipping his brush into the container, he asked casually, "Doesn't she have anyone to help her around the ranch?" She'd been out there over an hour, and from what he'd seen, she was doing everything herself.

"Sure," Elliot answered cheerfully, his eyes following the small, even strokes of the brush as Max coated the bone. "She has me."

Max grinned, retiring the brush and carefully screwing on the top of the metal container. "I meant besides you, Elliot."

Elliot paused, trying to recall the name of the man who worked for his aunt. He'd been hired at the end of last summer, just as Elliot was leaving. "Diego." He grinned, pleased that he remembered. "When he's here." He shifted out of the way as one of the students approached Max. "But he's not."

"That'll be ready to be wrapped for shipping in about fifteen minutes," Max told the student, carefully handing over the fragment. The student took it almost reverently, holding it by the edges of the cardboard where it rested. Max looked at Elliot. "Where is he?"

Elliot pushed his glasses impatiently back up his nose. "Aunt Rikki said she gave him the week off." A noise from the excavation caught his attention, and he moved to the edge to see what was happening. "He's got a sister in Mexico and she was getting married, so—"

"Your aunt let him go with all the work she has to do?" Max questioned over his shoulder. It didn't seem very logical to Max, what with the concern Rikki had for the horses and the amount of work that needed to be done around any ranch.

"That's what Mom asked. But Aunt Rikki said something about families needing to be together to celebrate important things."

An odd expression had come over the boy's features. Max couldn't help wondering what was going on in his head. "Thoughtful lady, your aunt."

"Yeah." Elliot abandoned his absorption with the excavation and crossed back to Max. He leaned his elbows on the table, resting his head on his upturned palms and looking into the man's face. "You like her?"

The question came totally out of the blue and caught him unprepared. Julia, within earshot, didn't quite manage to hide a grin behind the hand she suddenly passed over her face. "Yes," Max answered slowly, "I like her."

Elliot took in the information and nodded, pleased. "That's good."

Max rose from the table. This was a subject, he figured, that was better discussed in private. He placed his hand on Elliot's shoulder and led him to a slightly less populated area. Glancing over his shoulder, he saw Julia mouthing "Spoilsport," and grinning broadly. When they had first met, Julia had gone out of her way to fix him up with several of her friends. None of her efforts had led anywhere. He hadn't been interested. Now he was, almost against his own will.

"Why?" Max asked, trying to sound offhand about the question. Elliot's innocent expression dissolved any barriers he might have wanted to keep up.

"Because I think she gets lonely sometimes," Elliot answered honestly, his mind working through the situation. "Mom says every woman should be married, but Aunt Rikki says no."

Independent. She had struck him that way from the first moment she'd opened her mouth. Maybe that was what had intrigued him. That and a pair of violet eyes that threatened his inner core with total meltdown.

"Interesting." Max looked down at the boy's serious face. Elliot obviously had more thoughts on the subject.

"But I think maybe, sometimes, she'd like to say yes." Elliot peered up at Max to see if the man understood what he was trying to say. Satisfied, he went on. "Everybody needs somebody around to love them, huh?"

Max had once believed that, then changed his mind when it didn't appear that it would be his lot in life to meet anyone who fit that description. He had envied Allen his wife and children, but not to the point where it bothered him that he didn't have a family of his own.

"I suppose."

Elliot took that as a sign of agreement. "And I can't be here for her all the time. I only get summers off, you see." He took a deep breath and came in for his big finish. "I need someone here to take care of her. Aunt Rikki's very, very special."

A matchmaker. Apparently they came in all sizes. "How old did you say you were?"

"Nine. But I'm almost ten."

"When?"

"January," Elliot mumbled. He didn't quite know why he trusted Max not to laugh at him, the way some adults, like his mom's friends, had a habit of doing. But he did. A guy who admitted to wearing glasses when he didn't have to was okay in his book.

Seven months did not constitute "almost," but Max could relate to wanting to be older. He could remember when being twelve had seemed to be the most important thing in the world to him. The price of going to the movies went up when you turned twelve. He thought that meant being considered an adult. Eventually he'd learned that experience, the way you looked at things, made you an adult, not age. Some people never got there. In his estimation, Elliot was three-quarters there already. "Nine, huh? You sound more like thirty."

Elliot wasn't sure if that was a compliment or not. "Mom says I'm precocious."

Max had always hated that word. It made him think of a trained monkey performing before an audience at the circus. "I'd just say you were very bright. And sensitive."

Elliot grinned up at Max. He wasn't really sure about this sensitive stuff, but it seemed to him that Max thought it was okay, and that was good enough for him. He liked Max. A lot. He wondered if his aunt did. He thought so, but he couldn't be sure. Elliot decided that he would work on her when he got the chance, just to help things along. It would be great to have a dinosaur man in the family. And he could talk to Max. Not like his dad, who always seemed to say, "Later," whenever he had something to tell him. Later never seemed to come.

Max could almost hear the wheels turning in Elliot's head. "C'mon, Elliot." He placed his hand on the boy's shoulder. "We'd better get back to work."

Elliot loved the way that sounded.

When Max told Julia he was taking a break half an hour later, she met his announcement with silent surprise written across her face. She put down her pencil. "Something wrong, Max?"

"No, I just thought I'd stretch my legs." It was a lame excuse, and they both knew it. It wasn't like him, but he was feeling restless. Maybe it was the prospect of the dig. They had already found three more fossils, an incredible stroke of luck in such a short time. The crew was beginning to grow enthusiastic that this might not be just another wild-goose chase. Logically this would have been the time to push on.

But he wasn't being logical right now.

Julia merely smiled. "Elliot, why don't you tell me what you think of these?" She beckoned the boy over to her table.

Elliot was quick to leave Max's side and join her. The look in Julia's eyes told Max she knew what he was thinking.

That made one of them, he thought, shoving his hands into his pockets as he wandered away. He had absolutely no idea why he was acting so foolishly when there was work to be done.

Two students stopped him to ask a question. He answered them quickly, realizing as he did so that he was impatient for them to leave. Another out-of-character reaction for him. But he had an overwhelming need to wander over to the stables to see what Rikki had been doing in there for so long.

What she was doing, from what he could see, was getting frazzled. Five of the horses were back in their stalls, and she was busy spreading straw in the last stall. He watched her work for a moment. She was obviously intent on her chore. It seemed like too much work for one woman. One person, he amended, instinctively knowing she would have corrected him if he had put it that way.

"Why don't you hire someone to do that?"

Rikki jumped, startled, and the pitchfork slipped out of her hands. She turned toward the doorway and saw that he was standing a few feet away from her, watching. She hadn't even heard him come in.

"That costs money." Rikki bent down to pick up the pitchfork. "Besides, I've already got one hired hand."

Max approached her slowly, as if he were treading on eggshells instead of fresh straw. In a way, he was. "Elliot said you let the man have some time off."

She liked the way he moved, cautiously, not barging his way in. He was a gentle man, she decided, wondering why she needed to categorize him at all.

"That's right." The words melted from her lips like dewdrops in the sun as she watched his hand move toward her head.

"You've got a piece of straw in your hair." His voice was whisper soft. It was a very simple gesture. There was no reason in the world why it should seem the least bit intimate to her. But it did.

Rikki found she was having trouble concentrating on anything but the gentle look on his face as she held her breath.

The straw fell from his fingers. "Can't you get anyone temporarily?"

What was the matter with her? Why was her heart hammering like that? Turning her back to him, she began plowing through the straw energetically, as if the action could somehow unscramble her pulse again. "I can handle it for a week." She stopped, looking over her shoulder. "Unless, of course, you're volunteering."

There was that smile again, the one that reached her eyes. The one that reached out to something small and lost within him. He tried to keep his mind on the conversation. "I'm afraid I can't. You've been lucky for me." That wasn't what he had meant to say. He had meant to say that the dig had proven to be lucky.

Rikki cocked her head. "Excuse me?"

The way she held her head reminded him of Elliot. They shared the same puzzled expression. "We just unearthed three more fossils."

"More bones?" Apprehension and, for some strange reason, happiness mingled within her. Why happiness, for heaven's sake? There was nothing to be happy about. This meant they would be staying, continuing to throw her ranch into an uproar. There was no reason for her to react with anything but annoyance. Maybe she *was* working too hard.

"More bones," Max echoed. It was all he could do to keep from tracing the outline of her mouth with his fingertips. He felt this incredible need to touch her skin. To see if it was as silken as it looked.

Rikki sighed, leaning on the pitchfork. "What does that mean, exactly?"

He grinned. "That means the dinosaur had more than one bone."

He was making fun of her, she thought. Rikki raised her chin. "I know that, I mean—do you think there might be a whole one down there?"

"Odds are against that," he told her honestly. Max saw relief enter her eyes. Would she be that glad to be rid of him? Of course she would. His crew was making things difficult for her. "But there might be." Relief faded from those violet depths. "I guess that puts us at odds, as well, doesn't it? I'm hoping for a whole dinosaur, and you're hoping that the rest of him is anywhere but here."

When he put it like that, he made her feel as if she was taking away a deprived child's only Christmas present. Rikki straightened her shoulders. No, she wasn't going to let her sentiments get the best of her this time. All her life her problem had been that she could always empathize with both sides of a case. It made her waver, not wanting to hurt anyone's feelings, even at the cost of her own. For once, she needed to stick to her convictions.

She looked up into Max's face, one hand still wrapped around the pitchfork for support. She wished he was a couple of inches shorter, or she was a few inches taller, so she wouldn't have to look up as much.

"It's just that I have a ranch to run and horses to take care of. Not to mention bills to pay. This is supposed to be a working ranch, and right now I'm the only one who's working. And if you stay here, disrupting everything, who knows when things will get back to normal?"

Was it money she was worried about? He wondered if he could juggle the budget around to cover any financial difficulties she might incur. "But you're a vet, too. That has to pay something."

An enigmatic smile played on her lips as she thought of the other ranchers. There had only been a few calls for her services so far. And as far as she knew, none of the animals were about to give birth. "The livestock around here seem to be incredibly healthy." As well as celibate, she added silently.

Resistance to her smile, and to other things, was decreasing at an incredible rate. "Must be the clean air."

There was something in his face that made her freeze where she stood. She couldn't even swallow. "Must be."

He noticed that one of the strands of her hair had loosened from her braid, and he tucked it behind her ear.

Hesitantly—she could see it in his eyes as well as in his motion—he touched her face. He looked so uncertain, as if he were doing something unfamiliar, experiencing something for the first time. It made the action all the more special. It came from the heart. It wasn't a calculated act intended for effect.

He saw something spring into her eyes. Something cloudy and dark. And tempting.

Then the next thing seemed to happen purely by outside design. Instinct. Automatic pilot. Or whatever it was that seemed to govern things that were completely beyond human control. At least, beyond his control. Max had no idea he was going to kiss her.

Until he did and realized how much he had wanted to.

Rikki had always thought that unbridled passion was supposed to be the thing that set off all the bells and banjos of popular fiction. Sweetness wasn't supposed to do it. And yet, she was hearing them as clearly as if they were there in the stable with her, instead of just in her head.

Neither was sweetness supposed to trigger a hunger within her, one that was born and suddenly grew into full-fledged adulthood within the space of an instant.

But it did.

The pitchfork fell with a soft thud at her feet as searing shafts of pleasure exploded within her. Rikki suddenly needed her hands free to grasp on to him, to steady herself. To assure herself that this was really happening. That he was real.

She tilted her head back, drinking in the pleasure. Wave after wave washed over her, leaving her breathless, reeling. The kiss drew her up on her toes, perhaps even off the ground, she wasn't sure. There didn't seem to be any ground beneath her feet, only strong arms that held her, at once protecting her and making her vulnerable. The gentle kiss had grown in power and scope, completely devastating her and reducing her to the consistency of ice cream left out in the sun.

The kiss deepened and the stable faded away, spinning off into oblivion as Rikki grasped the front of Max's shirt, clinging, afraid to let go for fear of falling.

Max was filled with the most incredible feeling, as if he had just discovered something exquisite, something that no one had ever come across before. She felt soft and warm and wonderful in his arms, like a bit of sunshine he had captured. He wanted to go on kissing her forever. As she moaned against his lips, he was completely at her mercy, mystified by the power she had over him.

How had this happened? *When* had this happened?

"Max! Come here. Now!"

They pulled apart instantly at the sound of Julia's voice, confused and stunned by the magnitude of what they had just experienced.

Max dragged air back into his lungs, trying to steady his breathing. He doubted that he ever would again. He ran the tip of his thumb over her bottom lip. "Scientifically," he said softly, "I'd say that comes under the heading of spontaneous combustion."

"Max!" Julia's voice grew louder and more urgent. They both looked toward the open doorway, but neither made a move toward it.

He could feel just the slightest tremor passing through Rikki. Reluctantly he dropped his hands from her waist. "That sounds like the voice of discovery calling." His own voice was still hoarse, still shaken. He couldn't think of anything except the fire her kiss had ignited. How had it gotten out of hand this way?

"That would make two discoveries in the space of a minute," Rikki murmured. She blinked, playing back the words in her head. She flushed and took a step away from him, then stopped abruptly, blocked. She had backed up against the stall. "What did I just say?"

Unable to resist, he slid the back of his hand along her cheek. He saw a spark of desire rise in her eyes before she banked it. Yes, it had happened.

"I'm not sure, but it sounded nice. Rikki, I—" He needed words, but he couldn't find any. There didn't seem to be anything available to him that would cover this sort of thing. And he had never been very good at verbalizing his feelings.

"Max, where *are* you?"

"He's in here!" Elliot called out as he bounced into the stable. "They found another bone," he announced to Max and his aunt. "A big one—oh!" He skidded to a halt, looking from Rikki to his new idol, clearly torn. His expression indicated that he had suddenly realized he was interrupting something, something new and important. As important as the discovery that was being made outside. "Um, I can tell Ms. Teasdale that you're busy, Max."

He'd been right about him. The boy *was* sensitive. Max wanted to put him at ease. To put himself at ease. "I'm not busy." Max crossed over to Elliot.

"He's not busy," Rikki said quickly. Their voices threaded together, and they both laughed self-consciously.

Elliot looked from one to the other again and then frowned. "Oh."

Rikki could have sworn Elliot looked disappointed. His newfound exuberance had faded. When had he grown so old? she wondered fondly. "Another bone?" she prodded, trying to refocus Elliot's attention on something less personal, less threatening. She needed time to herself.

"Yeah." The light reentered Elliot's eyes as he thought of the excitement just beyond the stable door. "C'mon." He grabbed Max's shirtsleeve and tugged him toward the entrance. He was acting, she thought in satisfaction, like a normal nine-year-old. Max seemed to be affecting more than just her.

Max turned to look at Rikki, but she already had her back to him as she picked up the pitchfork from where she had dropped it. He felt a sense of relief as he let Elliot lead the way out. Another discovery. He needed something to occupy his mind right now. What had happened between him and Rikki was totally disconcerting and he needed time to think about it. He was in no condition to even begin to intelligently analyze what had just happened in the stable at this moment. And he needed to analyze it if he was going to live with it.

Something told him that he was going to have to figure out a way to live with it, or run the risk of losing a rare find.

"So, is anything interesting happening?" Virginia asked cheerfully, looking at Max across the dining room table. She had on a moss green dress that would have been more suited to a party. It looked out of place amid the casual clothes the others wore. Virginia didn't seem to notice.

Rikki glanced at Max. Yes, something interesting was happening, she thought, but not in the way Virginia meant. Then again, knowing Virginia, maybe it *was* the way Virginia meant it.

Her mind had been on their kiss ever since that morning. It had haunted the rest of her day like a melody that refused to leave no matter how hard you tried to find something to replace it.

"We found more bones!" Elliott announced with pride.

"You mean that the professor did, Elliot."

Max saw the patronizing look Virginia gave her son and came to the boy's rescue. "Actually, I wasn't there for the big find. I was somewhere else. Occupied." Without meaning to, his gaze drifted to Rikki.

"Oh?" Virginia said.

"What kind of bones are they?" Rikki asked hastily before Virginia could ask any more annoying questions.

Max paused. He had forgotten how good a home-cooked meal could taste. Mostly he lived on TV dinners. He savored a tender piece of meat before he answered. "Part of a jaw."

He sounded so positive. When she had stopped by earlier to see what all the excitement was about, it had looked like any other piece of a bone, except that it was petrified. "How can you tell?"

"Years of study," he answered solemnly. And then he smiled. "It gives me a fifty-fifty chance of guessing right."

He had a sense of humor. That was nice, Rikki thought. A lot of things about the man were nice. But for all she knew, she reminded herself, he could have nine children and a nice pregnant wife waiting somewhere. She knew absolutely nothing about the man she had kissed this morning.

Except that she hoped there weren't nine children or a pregnant wife somewhere. She looked up from her plate and saw that he was looking at her as if he knew what she was thinking.

She searched for something to ask. "Are you hoping to put together a *Brontosaurus?*"

"*Apatosaurus,* Aunt Rikki," Elliot corrected, moving a green stalk around his plate with his fork. He wondered how much broccoli he had to eat in order not to hurt his aunt's feelings.

Rikki looked at him. "A what?"

Max was about to interject, then decided to let Elliot elaborate instead. It would give him confidence, he thought. He nodded when Elliot glanced at him.

"*Apatosaurus,*" Elliot repeated. "It's not called a *Brontosaurus* anymore."

Rikki got a kick out of the way information rolled off Elliot's tongue. She leaned her elbow on the table, her fingers effectively hiding the smile that came to her lips. "My mistake."

"A lot of people make it," Max explained. "*Brontosaurus* was the most commonly identified dinosaur. The name actually means thunder lizard. But it was erroneously tagged and..."

Max leaned back, getting comfortable with his topic. He could talk about dinosaurs for hours. One story led to another, stories that held Elliot enthralled and even seemed to capture Virginia's attention. Rikki was surprised and amused by her sister's reaction. Virginia was used to being the center of attention. But Max's manner was so engaging, it was hard to resist.

Max himself, she thought, was hard to resist.

Rikki wondered, as she listened, if Max knew how charming he was. She somehow doubted it. He was very unassuming. That was part of his charm.

Rikki sat and took everything in, delighting in what was transpiring. It was the kind of dinner scene she always used to dream about, the kind of scene she had ached for as a child. The kind of scene she had been deprived of. Her parents had always taken their meals in the dining room while she and Virginia had eaten in the kitchen. If they ate together, it was because guests were present, and then they were expected to be quiet. Somehow she always failed to live up to their expectations and talked out of turn. Punishment had always followed those transgressions.

Someday, she mused, watching him, Max would make a very good father. He didn't take himself too seriously, only his work. It was easy to see that his work was magic for him. It was there in his eyes, in the way he looked whenever he spoke about it. It was his mistress, his lover, she thought with a sudden pang. Any woman who became interested in him would have some serious competition on her hands.

She was glad, she told herself as she rose to bring in the dessert, that she wasn't in the running for that position.

The sound of Max's laughter, melodic and genuine, followed her into the kitchen.

Chapter Six

Virginia elaborately retired her knife and fork across her plate, then smiled brightly, first at Max, then briefly at Rikki. "Why don't you two go outside and get some night air? It's lovely tonight. I'll take care of the dishes for you."

Rikki saw Elliot looking at his mother as if she had just announced she was from the planet Neptune. For a moment Rikki said nothing, attempting to regain enough composure to answer without laughing. Virginia? Work? The two words didn't belong in the same sentence. Possibly not in the same lifetime.

"Virginia," Rikki reminded her sister patiently, trying to recall if she had ever seen Virginia even pick up so much as a piece of clothing from the floor or rinse out a glass, "you don't know *how* to take care of the dishes."

Aristocratic shoulders lifted and fell indifferently. "What is there to take care of? I load them into the dishwasher, close the door and it does the rest." Virginia reached for her glass and began to rise from the table.

Rikki bit the inside of her cheek as she placed her hand over her sister's. "If I had a dishwasher."

Virginia froze and stared at her younger sister. "You don't?" There was horror in her voice, as if Rikki had just admitted to being a heathen.

"I don't," Rikki confirmed cheerfully.

If Virginia had paid any attention when she drifted through the kitchen in that detached, vague way she had around things that held no interest for her, she would have noticed that. Rikki wondered if Virginia had taken in the fact that she didn't own a microwave either.

"So, if you will all excuse me..." Rikki rose to her feet, taking Virginia's dish and placing it on top of her own.

Max rose as well, taking a dinner plate in either hand. "Need help?"

Virginia smiled and nodded, evidently pleased, Rikki noted. This was probably even better than her sister had hoped for. She and Max would be alone together, and Virginia wouldn't have to lift a finger.

Content, Virginia turned toward her son. "Come along, Elliot." She removed the two glasses he was holding in his hands.

Elliot looked at his mother, confusion apparent in his gaze. "But I want to help Aunt Rikki."

"You'll help by coming along," Virginia told him firmly.

Rikki didn't know whether to be touched by Virginia's almost-heroic sacrifice in volunteering to do the dishes or be utterly embarrassed by her sister's obvious maneuverings. The latter won. She closed her eyes for a minute as Elliot and Virginia left the room, searching for strength.

When she opened them again, she was looking into Max's face. Max's smile. It had the ability to warm her even as it struck her as utterly guileless. Somehow his smile seemed to make everything better. She had a feeling that he was more amused than embarrassed by what had just transpired. Thank heaven for small favors.

He pushed the swing door open for her with one hand, holding it as she passed through. He followed in her wake, still holding the dishes he had picked up.

"You really don't have to do that." Rikki nodded at the plates in his hands as she deposited her own in the sink.

Max moved aside an empty pot on the counter next to Rikki and set down the dishes he was holding. "You didn't have to feed me."

She tried to sound casual as she shrugged off the invitation. "Virginia would have had a heart attack if I didn't."

A strand of hair fell across her face, and he almost reached over to brush it aside. He liked looking at her. "Was that the only reason I was invited? To keep Virginia happy?"

"No, I—" She turned on the water, looking for the right words to use and still exit with grace. There didn't seem to be any. She had invited him because she had wanted to. There was no getting around that. Virginia could have had all the "heart attacks" and tantrums she wanted to. If Rikki hadn't wanted Max at her table, he wouldn't have been there. She kept her face forward, avoiding his gaze. "It was the neighborly thing to do, seeing as how you were once a neighbor here." She hoped her excuse wasn't too transparent.

Max allowed her the lie. "Oh." He crossed back into the dining room to gather the rest of the dishes. Loaded down, he used his back to push the door open again. "What made you move out here?"

She could tell by his expression that she really hadn't fooled him. "I wanted to get away from the madding crowd." A whimsical smile played over her lips as she began to submerge the plates into the foaming dishwater. She thought of the excavation crew practically at her doorstep. "Seems the madding crowd has followed me."

Max brushed against her shoulder as he slipped two glasses she'd neglected into the water. "Maybe not for long."

There was a slight pang she tried not to notice. "You mean if you don't find anything beyond what you've uncovered so far?"

He watched her hands as she washed. They moved quickly, deliberately. They were clever, capable hands, despite being so delicate. He wanted to feel them against his skin, the same quick, deliberate strokes feathering along his back. "Yes."

Rikki slipped a dripping dish into the rack. "Does that happen often?"

Max looked around for a towel. "Too often."

"Over there, by the refrigerator." She pointed for his benefit, suds dripping from her fingertip. Max took the towel from the counter and began to dry the first plate. Rikki tried not to think about how domestic this all seemed. How right. "What do you do then?"

Max leaned his hip against the counter as he reached for the next dish. "Look for another find." He smiled wistfully as he wiped. "Hope for another find."

Another find in parts unknown. Rikki shook her head. Even the thought of it depressed her. He would never be one to stay put. "Sounds like a pretty nomadic life to me."

He rubbed the same spot on the plate as he studied her face. "You say it as if it's a bad thing."

She looked up at him, their eyes meeting, each seeing something they hadn't noticed before. Something different. "Isn't it?"

"No." Though he said it mildly, there was feeling behind it. "It's exciting." He remembered his life before he had begun his work. "Being stuck in one place is what's bad."

She had no idea why she wished he didn't feel that way. People were entitled to their preferences. "Is that why you left?"

"That and other things."

But he didn't want to talk of other things with her. The reason why he had actually left was a closed subject, except that it had taught him a lesson. He knew now that he was meant for the kind of life he had chosen, not for a home and hearth. Which was fine with him. Or so he had felt before violet eyes had seeped into his consciousness.

He let the dish he was wiping join the others in the stack with a clatter. He winced, checking it over for a crack. Finding none, he offered her a sheepish grin.

There was something adorable about him, both boyish and yet manly at the same moment. "The quest for your own dinosaur," she guessed.

It had been more than that, but he didn't bother to correct her. "Yes."

Rikki sighed. She was so deep in thought that she didn't notice it. But he did.

They were such different people, she thought with more than a touch of sadness. Very different. They were of two distinct worlds and times, both literally and otherwise. She spent her time with live animals, he with reconstructing dead ones. He hated roots, and roots were all she had wanted, ever since she could remember. He lived for the past and she for the present.

And neither would have a future, she told herself. At least, not together.

Max watched the furrow deepen across her brow. She had stopped washing. "Something wrong?"

"No." Self-consciously, she pulled a handful of utensils into the water. Islands of suds had already formed, drifting apart. They thinned even more as she worked. "I'd, um, like to apologize for my sister." The smile she flashed him was tinged with chagrin. "Subtlety is not exactly her long suit."

"There's nothing to apologize for. The meal was good and the company was excellent."

He reached to take the utensils from her hand as she was about to place them on the rack. Their hands touched. Rikki wondered how she could keep her other hand in the water and not get electrocuted.

"It still is," he added.

When he looked at her like that, she felt completely nude, even though his eyes were only on her face. A flutter started in her stomach and reached her breasts, making everything tighten like the taut strings of an instrument waiting to be strummed.

She had to stop this. He would be gone, probably within the month, and besides, she knew absolutely nothing about him. She could be having these "electrical impulses" about an ax murderer, for heaven's sake. She wasn't behaving rationally.

It was something, she recalled dryly, her parents had often accused her of.

His face was lowering toward hers. Rikki felt her breath stop. Mayday! "Are you married?"

The question, coming out of the blue, just as he was about to kiss her, threw him completely. More than that, it offended him. Just what did she think of him? "I kissed you," he pointed out.

Was that supposed to be an answer? It sounded like an evasion to her. Why did he look so annoyed? Was he hiding something after all? "Married men kiss women other than their wives."

"I don't." That hadn't come out right. His momentary anger had words scrambling in his head. "I mean, I wouldn't, if I were married. Which I'm not." He was tripping over his own tongue. It happened frequently when he wasn't talking about subjects dealing with his chosen field. And this was as far off the beaten path as it could get for him. He thought of Sally. "I was engaged once. Does that count?"

She realized she had offended him and felt both contrite and oddly touched by his reaction.

"Only if you want it to." Did he? Had he loved someone else, kissed someone else the way he had her? Of course he had. What was wrong with her? It was only a kiss, for heaven's sake. Why was she mooning over something that happened every second somewhere in the world? A kiss wasn't unusual.

But his had been. For her.

"I don't."

She thought she saw just the slightest flutter of emotion in his eyes before it faded as he answered. Pain? Hurt? Or just dismissal? She wanted to know without knowing why.

"What happened?"

He reached for the last pot, a disparaging smile on his lips. He bore Sally no animosity. It had all turned out for the best. They hadn't been right for each other. He could see that now. He hoped she was happy, wherever she was. "She said I was too dull."

The man who had taken her into his arms in the stable this morning and kissed her senseless was anything *but* dull. "Did you kiss her?"

A little of Sally's criticism seemed to have stuck with him after all, he thought, wondering if Rikki took him for a total dolt, as well. "Yes, I kissed her." But there had never been any magic, he thought.

It didn't make sense to Rikki. She drew the last pot out of the water, then turned to look at him. "And she still thought you were dull?"

He liked her implication. Liked the way she studied him. His response came out on its own, only managing to surprise him afterward. "It wasn't the same as it was with you."

A sunbeam shone through her. "Why?"

He laughed as he dropped the wet towel on the counter. The maneuver brought him closer to her—as he had meant it to. "Do all vets tend to be this analytical?"

Rikki turned and found she had very little space left to her. Her back was to the sink. And Max was right there in front of her. "I don't know. I'm the only vet I really know."

Unable to resist any longer, he pushed aside the strand of hair from her face. "Doc Wilson never was. Analytical," he added as an afterthought.

She could feel his breath on her face. The muscles of her stomach began to tighten again, waiting. "Did you kiss him, too?"

"No." He laughed.

If he didn't kiss her soon, she was going to take the initiative. "Maybe that's why," she said.

His smile faded as a serious look entered his eyes. "Could I kiss you again?"

Bingo. Rikki felt her pulse begin to throb in her throat. What a stupid place for a pulse, she thought. It made swallowing so hard, and her mouth was dry. "If you feel you have to," she whispered.

He saw the amusement in her eyes. And the desire. "This is purely for scientific purposes, you understand. A comparison."

"To what?" Her mouth grew drier, and she wondered how she was forming any words at all.

Max slipped his hands around her waist, drawing her closer to him. It was, he thought, a perfect fit. So few things in nature were. "To this morning."

"I've never stood in the way of science before. It's too late to start now." She threaded her arms around his neck. She had to rise up on her toes to do it.

His body pressed against hers, lean and hard, and her pulse hammered harder, making Rikki aware of her own body at the same time. Awareness faded as his mouth lowered to hers.

She was certain she was braced for what was coming. Forewarned was forearmed.

It didn't make a bit of difference.

If anything, his kiss rocked her even more than before, because she thought she knew what was coming. She didn't. Neither one of them did. The force of the passion that erupted beneath the thin veil of sweetness had them reeling in surprise.

And fear.

He didn't know how to handle this. His entire life had been predictable, plotted. The unexpected came only from excavations, from things found in the ground. Tangible things. He could touch them, see them. This was something ethereal, at once elusive, delicate and so overwhelmingly binding that he didn't know if he could ever work his way free again. Her kiss, the feeling it created, sucked him into a vortex where he had to fight just to catch his breath, never mind his thoughts. Those were scattered to the four corners of eternity, deserting him and leaving him a mass of emotions and needs. Leaving him a total stranger to himself.

Rikki had never had a lasting relationship. The simple reason was that there had never been anyone who raised her emotions to a boiling point. Until now. There had been plenty of infatuations. To a one, they had always been interesting, stirring—and fleeting. She had never come close to anything like this, and it left her, at age twenty-eight, as defenseless as a young girl.

And as hungry as a woman.

His lips, hot, arousing, slid over her face. Her eyes fluttered shut as her limbs became more and more fluid. His very breath excited her as it drifted along her skin. Rikki dug her fingers into his shoulders as her head dropped back and she moaned.

"I think I'm suffocating," he murmured. With an effort, he drew his mouth away before more things happened that he couldn't control. Things that carried consequences.

She dropped her hands from his shoulders numbly. "That makes two of us." It was all she could manage before the last shreds of her breath gave out. She needed oxygen. There was no point in pretending. Max would know it was a lie. She took a deep breath, wondering when her pulse would get back to normal. "So, how did the experiment go?"

He smiled down into her face, framing it between his hands. He wanted to kiss her again, but he stopped. He didn't trust himself at the moment. Temptation was too great, and the price too high to pay, at least for now.

"I don't know. It seems that the test tube has exploded and the entire lab is in shambles."

"Maybe." Rikki's voice cracked. She cleared her throat and tried again. "Maybe the two chemicals shouldn't be mixed."

Was that how she felt? He tried to read her feelings in her eyes and found that he wasn't versed in things like that. He could only read signs left by past generations in the ground.

"Maybe." Max released her slowly. "Well, I have to be up early in the morning."

"How early?" she called after him as he headed toward the back door. She had hurt his feelings; she could detect it in the way his jaw tightened slightly. She hadn't meant to. She had only meant to protect her own.

Max stopped, his hand on the doorknob. "Five o'clock. Daybreak."

"Me too." Rikki searched for something to make amends. "Care for breakfast?" It was weak, but it was a start.

His answer came without thought. "Julia is—"

"Seeing to that," Rikki concluded for him. She raised her head a little defensively. "Was she the one you were engaged to?" The question slipped out without her meaning it to.

"Julia?" He laughed, trying to imagine that. He'd known Julia for almost five years, and she was like the sister he had never had. There had never been a moment when he had considered her in any other light. He had even given her away at her wedding last year. "No. It was someone else."

He shoved his hands into his pockets, withdrawing slightly. "Julia's the best draftswoman around, not to mention that she doubles as a photographer whenever our budget gets tight. And she always knows where to get her hands on willing students. I don't know what I'd do without her." He realized that his enthusiasm for Julia wasn't going over all that well. But he couldn't be anything if he couldn't be honest.

Maybe it was better this way. The less their paths crossed, the easier it would be to forget that her insides turned to mush when he kissed her. "Then you'll be having breakfast with her."

Breakfast was the time when they all talked over the morning's plans, when things seemed to be at their freshest. "No." Discussions could always be taken care of beforehand. Or after. He found himself wanting to eat his breakfast sitting opposite fascinating violet eyes. He grinned at her, knowing he wasn't being sensible, and mystified by his own behavior. "I'll be having breakfast here, if the invitation still holds."

A warm flutter rushed over her. So much for thinking that it was better if he took his meals elsewhere. "Why shouldn't it?"

"I don't know. You just had a funny look on your face for a second. I thought maybe you'd changed your mind." He wasn't any good at this, he thought. He had always felt honesty was the best way to proceed. Male-female relationships required too much time and effort. Understanding mysterious traces left in the ground by vanished species was a lot easier.

And yet . . .

"I always eat breakfast," Rikki said a little too casually, trying to deny the happy surge she felt. "Most important meal of the day." And it had just gotten more so.

He laughed as she parroted the old adage. "My sentiments exactly."

She matched his smile. "At least we agree on that."

He shrugged, anticipation taking hold of him, the way it did when he was on the brink of a new discovery. He had a feeling that what was between them went beyond their philosophy on breakfast. "There might be other things we agree on." He looked at her meaningfully, though he stayed where he was. "If we try."

The look in his eyes told her that he was thinking about the same thing that was on her mind. "You mean beyond kissing?"

He liked her straightforward approach to things. He related to it. "You never know. Stranger things have happened."

It made her smile even though she knew that somewhere down the line, very soon, there would be a rift. What they wanted out of life was too different for there not to be. For the time being, though, she could enjoy this temporary aberration in her life. This very pleasant aberration.

Rikki watched him leave, wondering how he would like being referred to as an aberration. He probably wouldn't care for it.

But that was all he could be, she told herself firmly, grabbing a stack of dishes. Carefully she placed them in the cupboard closest to her.

By definition, digs tended to go on in out-of-the-way places. She had no interest in pulling up stakes time and again and going to who-knew-where. Her whole childhood had been spent that way, flitting from one place to another, never really being able to call any one place home. She had hated it.

Rikki ran her hand along the counter slowly. This was what she loved, what she wanted. Something solid. Something that was there year in, year out. A community she could be part of.

She sighed and shook her head. Two completely different worlds.

"Well, how did it go?"

Virginia's voice disturbed her train of thought. Rikki looked up to see her sister sauntering into the kitchen.

Rikki frowned slightly, clearing her mind. She might have known Virginia would come swooping down as soon as he left. "He dries dishes very well."

Virginia crossed her arms in front of her, clearly displeased. "And nothing else?"

Rikki shoved a drawer closed a little too firmly. She knew what Virginia was after, but she didn't feel like sharing this, not yet. It was too new, too uncertain. Too precious. Besides, Virginia would have her married and on her honeymoon within the week if she gave the slightest indication that she liked Max. And for all the wrong reasons. Rikki didn't want to have a man just to have a warm body next to her at night. She wanted a whole host of things in the package. Love, commitment. And roots.

"No." She watched Virginia's eyes light up in anticipation, waiting for her to elaborate. Rikki obliged. "He stacks them pretty well, too."

"Erikka!"

She knew it was silly, but Rikki relished her tiny moment of victory. Right now, she was in absolutely no mood for Virginia's version of the Spanish Inquisition. She doubted she would ever be.

"Virginia, I'm going to look in on the horses." Rikki hung her apron on a hook and turned to look at her sister. "Care to join me?" she asked innocently.

Virginia looked at Rikki, stunned and more than a little annoyed at Rikki's lack of cooperation. "You must be joking."

"Yes, I guess I must be." Rikki tried to hide her smile as she crossed to the door. "See you later."

With that, she left the house, Virginia audibly muttering something about stubborn mules.

Chapter Seven

The spoon Rikki had been holding fell to the counter with a thud as she swung around from the pot boiling on the stove. She didn't feel the hot steam rising from the uncovered broth. Instead a strange coldness had seized her in its grip. She stared at the florid-faced squat man in her kitchen. "You're kidding."

Whitecastle shook his head slowly. "Wish I were."

He didn't look anything of the kind. Rikki dried her hands on the back of her jeans and flew out through the back door. Behind her, Whitecastle struggled to keep pace. Normally she would have let him catch up, not wanting to hurt his pride, but this time she ignored him. This was more important than pride. Rikki had to see for herself. This had all the markings of déjà vu, recreating a scene from two weeks ago. But this time she was really worried.

"Maybe it's a chicken bone." But even as she said it, she knew she was grasping at straws.,

"This baby ain't no chicken bone," Whitecastle huffed. "It's bigger'n the other one. Why are we runnin'? It's not going anywhere."

And neither is my life, if this keeps up, she thought, without breaking stride. She left Whitecastle far behind. Two foundations, two finds. This just wasn't fair. Other people had foundations sunk, and they never came up with anything except dirt and rock. Why did this keep happening to her?

By the time she reached the site of the new stable, her anger was boiling the same way the pot on her stove was. Max was already down in the hole. Naturally. The expression on his face told her everything.

Perfect. Just perfect.

Whitecastle jostled her slightly as he stopped next to Rikki at the perimeter of the new excavation. He peered down at Max. "Looks like this was a big fella, all right." Whitecastle scratched one of his never-ending itches as he regarded the latest find.

Rikki looked down at Max, who looked as happy as a child granted permanent recess from school. "Is it part of the same dinosaur?"

Max looked up. Was that anger in her voice? "Hard to tell right now." He glanced down at the bone, which was only half exposed. "Maybe part of the same one, maybe another one."

Rikki stifled a huff as she placed clenched fists on her hips. More time wasted. And the horse auction was getting closer all the time. "Don't tell me, let me guess. You want to set up a second dig here."

Her eyes were open wide, but this time he saw no humor in them. Max grinned sheepishly as he nodded. "You catch on fast."

This was too much. She couldn't afford to be magnanimous anymore. "Faster than that. The answer is no."

Max fairly vaulted out of the excavation. He placed his hand on her shoulder. "Rikki—"

She shrugged off his hand. "No." The word echoed emphatically. She shut out the surprised look on Elliot's face. It was hard enough dealing with Max's stunned expression.

Work stopped abruptly as everyone turned to look at her. The two sites weren't that far apart, and her single word had gained the attention of both Whitecastle's crew and Max's students. She felt like the villain in an old-fashioned melodrama. But this was her land, not a playground for paleontologists.

"I'm very sorry, Max, one dig is my limit." She threw her hands up in exasperation and began to walk away. She didn't want to cause a scene with everyone listening. She didn't want to cause a scene at all, but there didn't seem to be a way to avoid one. She and Max were obviously at loggerheads.

Max caught up with her quickly. He placed a hand on her shoulder, his grip firm. Rikki swung around, angry at him for putting her in a position she didn't want to be in.

"I have to put the horses into a permanent barn, Max. There are going to be more coming soon. What am I supposed to do with them if you dig here?" She gestured toward the site they had just left. "Put them up in the house?"

Max ran a hand through his hair, casting about for a solution. "You could choose an alternative site."

His voice was maddeningly low-key. She didn't want to be placated or patronized. "I already *chose* an alternative site. That one." She jerked her hand toward the large rectangular hole in the ground they had just left behind. "And one of your damn bones popped up."

How could he make her see reason? "They're not my bones. They belong—"

"I know, to everyone." Rikki blew out an impatient breath, catching wisps of hair in the gust. "Well, I make up part of that 'everyone,' and my vote is that I don't want another dinosaur in the world. I want my stable." She knew she sounded like a petulant child, but that couldn't be helped. She was striving to build something, not tear things down to reconstruct the past.

Taking a breath, she tried again. "All this costs money, Max." Money she didn't have. Ever since she had gone her own way, there had only been a small inheritance from her paternal grandmother to fall back on. And that was gone now. If she couldn't make her ranch pay, there would be no money at all. For that she needed breeding stock. And a place to put them when they arrived.

Max looked toward the site, then made his decision. "We'll absorb the costs."

In her head, she had been preparing for whatever arguments he was going to present, but she hadn't anticipated this. She opened her mouth, but nothing came out. Instead she blinked, trying to assimilate what he had just said. "What?"

Max could see the anger receding from her eyes already. She could be reasoned with. "If you're willing to move the site again, we'll absorb the costs. I can get funds allocated to have your stable built in time to house the new horses."

The wind had left her sails, but she wasn't totally subdued. She'd been burned once. Rikki folded her arms across her chest. "And if they find another dinosaur bone there?"

Unless some natural disaster had wiped out an entire herd of dinosaurs, he doubted that was possible. Lightning rarely struck twice, and never three times. "I don't think I'll be that lucky."

Rikki frowned, thinking. She didn't want to be pigheaded about this. She supposed she could pick a third site for the stable.

Whitecastle ambled over as if he had been invited to share the discussion, ignoring the looks that both Rikki and Max directed his way as he joined them. He scratched the white bristles on his double chin, making a raspy noise.

"You really don't have a say in the matter, you know." Rikki's head jerked around in time to catch the warning look that Max shot the older man. "What?" Whitecastle demanded in response to Max's scowl. "Doesn't she know?"

Rikki's eyes narrowed. "Know what?" She directed her question to Max.

He turned away. "Nothing."

She grabbed Max's arm for emphasis. She wasn't about to be lied to or toyed with. "Know what?" she repeated forcefully. She didn't like being kept in the dark about anything, good or bad.

Whitecastle gave Max a chagrined look before answering. "Law's on his side." He nodded at his own words. "You don't own the mineral rights to your land. If he thinks there's something down there to benefit the public, he's got the right to go ahead. Dinosaur digs take precedence over ownership."

Rikki turned to see Elliot joining them hesitantly. Because of him, she kept her anger in check. In the space of two weeks her "little old man" had been transformed into a lively, chattering little boy. She didn't want to jeopardize that by making him feel he had to choose between them in this argument. "Is this true, Max?"

"I would have put it better." The look in her eyes pinned him down. "But, yes."

He had been laughing at her, playing the begging paleontologist coming to her hat in hand, making her believe she had the final word. She hated being made a fool of. "Then why all the diplomacy?"

He saw something dark rising in her eyes. Why? "It's your land. I didn't want to muscle in. I would rather have done this with your permission."

"Well..." She shoved her hands into her pockets, searching for words, trying not to explode. Once again things were beyond her control. On her own land. Frustration licked at her. "You obviously don't need it. Go ahead and dig."

She turned on her heel, walking away from them quickly. She knew she wasn't acting like a clear-thinking adult, but she was angry. This was her land, her property. She kicked a rock out of the way. She was trying to build a future for herself, but he didn't care about futures, hers or anyone else's. All he cared about were his lousy dinosaurs. She was a fool to have believed anything else. It had all been an act to get his dig underway without having to put up with any problems from her.

Well, he had underestimated her. Maybe she couldn't stop him, but she wasn't going to make this easy. Kiss her until she was senseless, would he? He was going to pay for that.

Max watched Rikki walk away. The set of her shoulders told him in no uncertain terms exactly what she was feeling. Strange how he seemed to be able to read her moods when he had never been able to fathom anyone else's.

Julia approached him from behind and tapped him on the shoulder. "Max, I—"

Whatever it was, it was going to have to wait. "Take over, Julia." He hurried after Rikki. "Rikki!"

Rikki kept walking, refusing to answer. She had to cool down first and regain her composure. She felt angry tears stinging her eyes. She didn't want to cry, to let go of the emotions churning within her. Tears were always seen as a sign of weakness. Why did they always have to surface and betray her just when she wanted to put up a strong front?

Max caught up to her just before she walked into the old stable. He tried to grab her shoulder.

Rikki shrugged him off, just as she had before. She didn't want to talk to him anymore. There were too many emotions colliding inside her, emotions she was afraid of turning loose. "Go away and play with your dinosaurs, Max." It was all he cared about anyway, wasn't it? Kissing her had just been his method of getting his way. The thought hurt.

"Rikki, grow up." He had absolutely no idea where that had come from. It took them both by surprise and shocked Rikki enough to make her swing around to glare at him.

"Grow up? *Grow up?*" she echoed incredulously. How dare he? "I'm the one trying to build a life here. All you want to do is play with dinosaur bones like a little boy." She knocked away his hand as he raised it toward her. She didn't want him touching her. Contact would weaken her resolve. "Maybe if you keep digging in the past enough, you won't have to face the future.

You're escaping, Max. I'm trying to live. You live in the past to escape the present.''

He looked at her, not knowing what to make of what he saw in her eyes. He'd been wrong when he thought he knew how her mind worked. He didn't have a clue. ''What are you talking about?''

She hadn't meant to say what she had. It had just come tumbling out on the heels of her hurt pride. ''I don't know.'' She looked away. ''I don't like being kept in the dark.''

Gently, one hand on her shoulder, holding her in place, he raised her chin with his forefinger, forcing her to look at him. ''And I don't like having to strong-arm people to get my way.''

He wasn't going to get around her with kindness. She refused to give up her anger. ''Isn't that what you're doing now?''

He dropped his hand from her shoulder. ''Do you want me to leave?''

''Yes!'' She took a deep breath, her voice lowering. ''No.'' Though she had nothing to base it on, she suddenly felt that, despite what Whitecastle had told her, Max would leave if she told him to.

''What *do* you want?'' Max asked softly. He saw the turmoil in her face.

''I want my life back,'' she answered quickly. ''The one I was building. I want peace and quiet. I want—'' It wasn't so easy anymore. The game plan had been altered. ''I want you to stop haunting my mind.''

His hands were back on her shoulders, as if that could somehow help him understand what she was saying to him. ''What?''

She hadn't wanted to admit that once, much less twice. ''You heard me.''

Max shook his head. "I'm not sure about that. It sounded as if you said I was on your mind." A smile began to lift the corners of his mouth.

His smile was infectious, even when she tried to block it. "'Haunting my mind' was the term." She looked at the expression on his face and pretended to be indignant. "What are you grinning about?"

He couldn't help it. "I never thought of myself as haunting anyone before."

She couldn't think of a way to lie her way out of this. "Well, you have been." Since she was being truthful, she might as well go all the way. "And I don't want you to."

"Why?" he asked, intrigued.

Her eyes grew serious as her voice softened. "Because when this is over, you'll be gone, off to another dig or whatever."

He didn't know when her hand had come between both of his. It felt soft and smooth, despite all the work she did, and he realized that he wanted to go on holding it for a long time. "You could come with me when I go."

Rikki shook her head. "No, I don't think so."

He didn't see the problem. She was free to pick up and go if she wanted to. "Why not?"

"Because I want to feel like I belong." She searched his eyes, knowing he didn't understand, wishing that he did, that he could feel the way she did. "I spent a lot of years living out of a suitcase, and I don't want that kind of a life again. I want a white picket fence."

He glanced back at the house to reinforce his assessment. "You don't have that now."

She smiled. Leave it to him to be so literal. "Diego will build one for me this winter. I want a family." Her voice took on an urgent note as she tried to make him see. "Thanksgiving turkey. A small-town life. I don't want to have to wake up in the morning trying to remember where I am.''

The pain in her voice was hard to overlook. ''Was that what it was like when you were growing up?'' Max asked gently.

''Yes.''

''Army brat?''

She shook her head, feeling slightly silly. ''Hardly. Underprivileged rich kid.''

Because she looked as if she wouldn't shrug him off this time, he put his arm around her shoulders. ''Isn't that an oxymoron?''

''Not really. At least, not in my case.'' An enigmatic smile slowly filtered across her lips. ''My mother had breeding, my father had money and wanted breeding. They spent—and probably *are* spending, even as we speak—all their time enjoying the good life. At least, that's how they see it.'' She stopped and thought for a second. ''I think they're in France now. Maybe Athens.''

She was such a warm person that her lack of parental ties surprised him. ''You don't keep in touch?''

It had been her parents' choice, not hers. ''I'm the black sheep. People don't stay in touch with the black sheep.''

He thought she was painting too dark a portrait. ''Your sister did.''

''That's only because she needed somewhere to go.'' She wished it were otherwise, but she wasn't blind to the truth. ''Don't get me wrong, I like being needed, but it would be nice not to be thought of as the odd one.''

He played with a lock of her hair. ''I don't think of you that way.''

All right, she thought, his kindness *had* gotten to her. "I didn't mean to fly off the handle that way before." She flushed. "It's just that—"

He placed a finger over her lips. "No apology necessary. I know what frustration feels like. It's the way I felt when I was living here."

She wished he hadn't come up with that comparison. They didn't have a prayer, she thought, listening to him. He had wanted out, and she wanted in.

He took her silence as understanding. "It was so confining, so predictable, here."

She pictured life the way he spent it now, shifting through sand, blasting through rock. "And dinosaur digs are exciting?"

"Yes." He said the word with zeal. "Do you know what it's like to hold a piece of the past in your hand? A piece of history?"

She could relate to the feeling, if not the source. "Probably something like holding a newborn colt," she murmured.

"Probably," he agreed. They shared the same feelings, the same sentiments. But about different things. He wondered if there was a resolution in the making anywhere, and if he had the right to even want one.

Behind them, Whitecastle's bulldozer had come to life and was plowing through another layer of earth. Max raised his voice to be heard. "I'll talk to Roger about moving the foundations for the stable again."

She didn't like not being able to pay her own way. "No, I—"

He wasn't going to get involved in another discussion. He had made up his mind. "I meant what I said about paying for it."

She had always heard that funds for these sorts of things were hard to come by. "Where are you getting the money for all this?"

"Partially museum funding."

"And partially?" she prodded.

"My own."

"I can't let you—"

"Yes, you can." There was no arguing with his tone. "I go a long way to maintain goodwill." He placed his hands on her shoulders and bent his head.

"I'll say." She rose upon her toes to meet his lips. It was a soft, fleeting kiss, sealing a bargain.

And possibly, Rikki thought, sealing a good deal more.

He couldn't sleep that night. There was too much to think about, too much to assimilate. Too much that concerned her.

Max paced around his small trailer, trying to sort out his thoughts. His path was impeded at every turn, literally and figuratively. From all the evidence that had been gathered in the past two weeks, this was definitely a fruitful find. Whether or not there was more to be unearthed remained to be seen, but as long as his resources held out, he was willing to stay here for the duration. He had lied about the money coming from the museum for the stable. That would be paid for out of his own pocket. It wouldn't have been right otherwise. Whitecastle had been a lifelong friend of his father's. Max had talked to him and "come to an understanding." The man was going to begin excavation on a third site tomorrow for a greatly reduced fee.

Third time was the charm, Max hoped. At least for her.

For him, it had come a lot sooner.

He looked out the window that faced her house, wondering if he would get any sleep tonight. That was when he saw her, flashlight in hand, hurrying to the stables.

She mothered those horses something fierce, Max thought. He decided that a little night air might help him sleep.

It was dark in the stable. The smell of horses, hay and liniment mingled around him. Max squinted to make out shapes. There was a light on at the far end. "Rikki," he called out as he approached. "I saw you going into the stable and—"

"Over here," she called.

The urgent note in her voice had him hurrying to the last stall. He found her on her knees, beside the mare. Rikki looked worried.

"Is it her time?"

Rikki shook her head. "No, she's early." She bit her lip. She didn't like this. Not at all. "Like the last time. I think it's all this commotion. It hasn't been good for her." There was no accusation in her voice. Just concern.

Max squatted down next to the mare's head. It wasn't the first time he had seen an animal in labor. He ran his hand lightly over the sleek neck. It was damp with sweat. "Can I do anything to help?"

Sugar jerked, trying to get back on her feet. "Keep her still."

"It'll be okay, Rikki."

"Sure it will." She said the words in order to hear them out loud. "I'm a hell of a vet." She flashed him a smile she didn't really feel. "I know this is going to sound like a cliché, but I need—"

"Hot water, towels and a blanket." Max gave her a mock salute, already on his feet. "Just tell me where everything is. I've been through this kind of thing before."

She had forgotten that he had grown up around here. He had probably witnessed birth more than she had. "There's a basin under the sink in the kitchen. Linen closet's right off the main bedroom. The door's open." She was talking to his back.

"I'm on my way."

After gathering the supplies, he returned to her side as quickly as he could. He noticed the deep furrow across her brow immediately. "What's the matter, wrong color?" He nodded at the blanket, trying to get a smile from her.

He didn't succeed in erasing the furrow. "The foal's in breech position. I'm going to have to turn it." She took a deep breath, bracing herself.

Having him there helped. It wasn't actually anything he said or did. It was just knowing he was there—for her.

Carefully Rikki placed her hands inside the horse, then moved them slowly up the birth canal. The mare jerked, trying to rise. There was panic in her whinny. Rikki looked over her shoulder at Max.

"I've got her." His muscles strained as he kept the animal steady. "Do what you have to." He watched as beads of perspiration gathered along Rikki's forehead, glistening before they slid down her temples, dampening her hair.

"It's okay, Sugar, it's okay." Rikki's voice was singsong as she tried to soothe the mare, all the while working to turn the small foal fighting to be born. "This isn't a picnic for either one of us, although around about now, I'm sure you'd like to trade places."

The horse made a noise that sounded like a human scream. Rikki drew back, afraid. "You can do it," Max said softly. The look on her face was so intense, he wondered if she had even heard.

She had. Bracing herself, she tried again. This time she felt the foal moving. "A little more, a little more," she murmured to the mare. The huge dark eyes watched her, and Rikki could have sworn the mare understood what she was saying.

Letting out a huge sigh, Rikki removed her hands and seemed to collapse for a moment.

"Rikki, are you . . ."

She lifted her head, the look on her face one of relief and hope. "I turned it." Tears shimmered in her eyes, falling into the perspiration on her cheeks. She leaned over Sugar. "C'mon, girl," she encouraged, patting the long, slender neck lovingly. "Your turn."

Max could feel every sinew on the mare tense. "She takes direction well."

"It's happening," Rikki cried, as excited now as she was the first time she had witnessed the miracle of birth. Each time was wondrous to her.

Two forelegs appeared. "Atta girl, you're doing it. It's coming. It's coming!"

Max watched Rikki, fascinated. It occurred to him that he had never seen a more beautiful woman in his life. Her cheeks were flushed with the glow of excitement.

"Max, I see the head. He's almost here, Sugar. Almost done. Oh, he's a strong one, girl. Look at him fight."

Rikki helped ease the shoulders out. The rest of the foal slid through easily.

"Done, girl!" After first cutting the cord that connected the two, Rikki wrapped the foal in the fresh towels, cleaning him off. "You've got a beautiful son, Sugar. You did good."

"And so did you." Max joined her, squatting down on his heels. The tiny life-form between them uttered a small, short whinny, and Rikki laughed, totally high on life.

"Isn't he just the most beautiful thing you've ever seen?" She drew the towels away.

"Handsome," Max corrected, admiration in his eyes for the woman before him. "Males are handsome. *You* are beautiful."

"I'm a mess." With only a small degree of self-consciousness, Rikki brushed her hair away from her face with the back of her hand.

"A beautiful mess." Unmindful of the mare and her new foal, Max drew Rikki to her feet and pulled her into his arms. "You were nothing short of magnificent."

"Sugar did all the work."

"I don't think so. Don't forget, I was here."

"Yes, you were."

There was no need for words, not right now. The communion they had shared, watching life coming into the world, was awe-inspiring and all that was necessary.

Max kissed her with feeling that he hadn't known was there until it erupted in his veins, feeling that seemed to have been lying dormant, waiting for the right woman, the right moment.

He felt like Adam, waking up to find Eve at his side, a gift from God.

A gift he was sure he would have willingly accepted, allowing him to reach paradise, had the new colt not bumped against them as he tried to rise to his feet.

The spell broken, Rikki turned and laughed as she looked down at the colt. "What did I tell you? He's a real little fighter."

Max had another word for him at the moment.

Chapter Eight

An incredibly cheerful tune from the forties filtered into the kitchen. Rikki winced. Bits and pieces of dialogue coming from the television seeped into the room each time there was a lull in the ruckus outside. With two digs going on, plus the construction crew in full swing, there were precious few lulls to be had. Why did they have to be filled with the noise of the television?

Just as Rikki had feared, "Baby" had been brought into action the first week, after Max decided that the site warranted major digging.

Rikki retrieved a handful of carrots from the refrigerator and began to quickly peel them. She glanced at the old clock on the wall. No matter what she did, it steadily lost time and was now five minutes behind. That was all right, she thought; that made her fifteen minutes behind schedule instead of twenty. She sighed and worked faster, the rhythm of her hands guided by the tempo of the music she was listening to against her will.

She frowned, remembering when Max had told her about putting the bulldozer into high gear. She had been upset but powerless and had resigned herself to the situation. There was nothing else she could do. Well, at least he had talked to her first.

It seemed to her, Rikki thought as she diced the carrots, that Max could probably talk people into a lot of things. He wasn't a con artist; he just had a manner that made people trust him. Sincerity, that was it. It seemed to come from his every pore.

Rikki raised the cutting board above the pot of water on the stove and tilted it. Carrots went sliding down, splashing as they made contact. She supposed that had been what made her fly off the handle when she found out he hadn't told her that he could dig on her property without her permission. She had felt he'd lied to her.

No, it wasn't a lie, just an omission. She wondered if there were other things that he had omitted telling her. Important things.

She opened a sack of potatoes. She was certainly spending a lot of time thinking about a man who was only passing through her life, she mused. She selected five large potatoes for the stew. That was the term for it, all right, passing through. They hadn't discovered another fossil for over a week, though digging on the two sites was going on at full steam. What if there were no more pieces of the dinosaur puzzle to be found here? He would leave, going on to the next horizon. He couldn't help himself. It was in his blood.

And she would stay here. Nothing unusual about that.

The only thing that was unusual was the way she felt when he kissed her. As if there was nothing else in the world except for the two of them. But that wasn't true. There were lots of other things, things like responsibilities and careers and a feeling of purpose. They were all there, clearly defined—when his lips weren't touching hers.

She sighed, quartered a potato and tossed it in with the carrots. In the background, someone was crooning about his undying love.

"Oh God, Virginia, get a life," she muttered. Rikki almost welcomed the sound of the digging in place of the bouncy, stilted dialogue and overdramatic melodies that punctuated the movies on afternoon television. When Virginia wasn't flirting with Max at the dinner table, she was sitting in front of the television, getting involved in other people's lives. Letting her own slip away.

A bright, breezy voice began expounding on the merits of some new detergent. Rikki rolled her eyes heavenward. Enough was enough. She elbowed open the swing door that separated the kitchen from the living room. Virginia was curled up on the sofa, a pillow tucked up behind her, her eyes almost glazed as she followed the action on the screen.

If she could get this involved in a detergent commercial, it was time for some drastic action.

"Why don't you go home?"

Virginia blinked and shook her head, as if she was coming out of a daze. It took her a full minute before she focused on Rikki, and she still didn't grasp what Rikki had just said. "What?"

"Go home, Virginia," she repeated softly. "To your life. Where you belong." She gestured around the room. "You don't belong here in the country without a country club attached to it."

Rikki smiled, thinking of all the time her sister had spent sunbathing by the pool at an endless string of country clubs, perfecting her tan and flirting. It wasn't the kind of life Rikki would have chosen on her own, but it had made Virginia happy.

Virginia sat up and gripped the sofa's arm. "Are you throwing me out into the street?"

Rikki crossed to her, then slowly removed Virginia's hand from the arm. She perched there instead. "No, I'm throwing you back into your nice estate." She smiled down at her, hoping to coax Virginia to talk. "You've been here three weeks, and I've been as patient as possible, but you still haven't told me what's wrong."

Rikki sighed. Virginia had said as much on the first day she had arrived and then mercurially chosen not to elaborate. Par for the course. "The only time you voluntarily come near an area that contains a horse is when there's a track in front of it and a loving cup at the end of the line. This isn't your regular stomping ground, Virginia. For you to even be here means that something's very wrong."

Virginia averted her head, looking at the television set again. Rikki took the remote control and snapped off the set just as someone broke into a soft-shoe. "Talk to me, Ginny. Virginia," Rikki amended for the sake of peace.

Virginia reached for the remote control, but Rikki raised it over her head. It was hard for Virginia to open up, especially about an area that she thought she had done so well in, a fact she was always bringing up to Erikka.

"Maybe I just want to spend some time with you and Elliot, go on a vacation with him." It was the excuse she had given Elliot when they came out. She raised her chin defensively. "He is my son, you know."

"Your *son* has been outside with Max for almost three weeks straight," Rikki pointed out. "I've been out working on the ranch. You have slept late, watched old movies and acted like Audrey Hepburn in *Sabrina* over dinner. That doesn't exactly come under the heading of togetherness in my book.''

Virginia's lower lip suddenly trembled. ''Well, *he's* not here.''

Rikki hadn't been prepared for that. There were tears in Virginia's eyes. ''Who?''

Virginia sniffed impatiently, wiping aside one errant tear. Tears were for getting her own way, not for acting like a fool in front of her less-privileged sister. ''Wallace.''

''No, he's not,'' Rikki agreed slowly, waiting for Virginia to continue so she could gain some clarity on the subject. The heart of the matter was there somewhere, if only she lived long enough to find it.

''He was supposed to come after me, to ask my forgiveness.'' Virginia fairly snapped out the words. She didn't like having to explain herself or her motives.

It was obvious that her sister had watched one too many musicals. ''Is this some kind of a game?''

''No! No,'' Virginia repeated, her voice softening. A note of sadness entered. ''It's not a game.''

Yes, it was, Rikki thought, if she knew Virginia. Somewhere in that fashion-filled head of hers, Virginia was waiting for Wallace to act like a knight in shining armor. ''Does Wallace know the rules, though?''

Virginia rose to her feet, restless. ''He doesn't love me!''

Rikki was trying to be impartial, but it was hard, hearing the pain in Virginia's voice. Whatever else went on between them, Virginia was her sister. ''Did he tell you that?''

The look Virginia gave her was one reserved for an addle-brained idiot. "He's not here."

"We're back to that again." Rikki sighed, trying to make some kind of sense out of all this. With Virginia, it was hard. "Did you two have a fight?"

Virginia began to deny it, then nodded. "Yes."

Rikki paused. She knew that Wallace and Virginia *never* fought. They were blandly compatible. "Was it about something big?"

"Yes." The answer was given grudgingly.

Rikki's patience snapped. "What?" she shouted at her sister, jumping to her feet.

"I caught him with another woman." Virginia turned her back on Rikki, afraid of seeing a smug look. After all, she was the one who was always flaunting her married state. And now that state had crumbled on her.

Wallace? The man who had mooned after Virginia for a year and a half before she agreed to marry him? Something didn't sound right. Rikki turned Virginia around to face her. "Caught him how?"

"Kissing her." Virginia spit out the words. "Although he said she was kissing him," she added in an offhand manner.

"Possibly," Rikki said slowly, contemplating the matter. As far as she knew, her brother-in-law wasn't a womanizer. He'd been the one to pursue Virginia. Every time she saw the two of them, Wallace had seemed happier with the union than Virginia was.

"How can you take his side?" Virginia wailed.

Rikki shook her head. Virginia didn't begin to understand anything. She had probably gotten the situation with Wallace muddled, as well. "I'm not taking anyone's side, I'm trying to get to the bottom of all this. Exactly what did Wallace say when you 'caught' him?"

"That she'd been throwing herself at him. That he had been caught off guard, and that I walked into his office just in time."

Now that sounded like Wallace. Why was it that she knew her sister's husband better than Virginia did? "Did it ever occur to you that he was telling the truth?"

Virginia laughed at the naiveté of the question. "He's a man."

Rikki wasn't about to be baited by the condescending look in Virginia's eyes. "Obviously, or you wouldn't be married. Men do sometimes tell the truth, you know."

But Virginia refused to be swayed. "Then why isn't he here?"

Rikki's patience was wearing thin. That always seemed to happen around Virginia, she thought, no matter how motivated by good intentions she was when she first began talking to her sister.

"Maybe because he was hurt that you ran off without believing him. Or maybe because he has no idea where you are."

"I left him a note."

"Which said . . ." Rikki prodded.

"That Elliot and I were going on a vacation."

Rikki threw up her hands. "Well, that narrows things down."

Virginia shook her head at the excuse. "He just doesn't love me anymore."

Rikki sighed. There was no talking to Virginia when she was like this. Rikki handed her the remote control and left the room. The musical was back on before the swing door had a chance to close.

It was time, Rikki decided, to meddle.

Ten minutes later, she replaced the kitchen receiver into the cradle and smiled to herself. Virginia would be on her way home soon. Whistling softly, Rikki picked up the paring knife and began to diligently make short work of the last potato.

Max walked in the back door unexpectedly. Rikki looked up, but continued cutting. Knife met thumb. She yelped.

"Damn." The potato fell to the floor and rolled under the table as she popped her thumb into her mouth. "Do you have to sneak up that way?"

Max bent over to retrieve the fallen potato. He stood with it in his hand, his attention focused on Rikki. "Walking in the back door in broad daylight when you're six-three is not called sneaking. Here, let me see that." He gently tugged her thumb from her lips, then frowned at the angry red line. "Don't you know it can get infected if you pop it into your mouth like that?"

Rikki tugged her hand away. "I'm a doctor. Of course I know."

He smiled at the trace of feistiness. "Physician, heal thyself. Where's your iodine?"

Rikki examined her thumb. It was going to sting like anything. The little cuts always did. "The physician wouldn't have to heal herself if people didn't keep walking in unexpectedly."

He looked down at her other hand. She was still clutching the knife. "I never argue with a woman who's holding a paring knife." Max took her hand in his again. "Let me see that," he insisted.

She didn't like being clumsy around people. "It's okay."

On examination the cut looked deeper than he'd first thought. "It's nasty."

She tried to tug her hand away again but found that he had a better grip on it this time. "So will I be if you don't stop fussing."

Max raised his eyes to her face. "You know what I think?"

She watched him reach for a paper towel, one hand still holding hers. "No, and I don't particularly want to know."

He grinned. She could be contrary when she wanted to. Any way he looked at it, he liked her spirit. "I'll tell you anyway. I don't think people have fussed enough over you."

He struck a nerve, a nerve she would rather have kept unexposed. "You don't strike me as the fussing type."

"I'm not." And he wasn't. Until now. But he liked doing things for her. It was something he was going to have to think about in the wee hours, when his mind was at its clearest.

She looked at the way he was drying her thumb with the paper towel. Gently. Carefully. "Could have fooled me."

He looked up again, his eyes holding hers for a moment. "I think I could have fooled a lot of people." Himself included.

The back door opened beneath Whitecastle's beefy knuckles as he knocked. He walked in, then looked from Max to Rikki, his eyes finally resting on their joined hands. "Am I interrupting anything?"

Nothing that shouldn't be interrupted, Rikki thought.

She couldn't keep reacting to Max this way. She definitely had to stop finding things she liked about him. His gentleness, his thoughtfulness. The sexy way he smelled.

Fat chance.

Max felt Rikki yank her hand again, but he held it firm. He watched a dot of blood materialize on the paper towel that covered her thumb. "I'm keeping the vet from bleeding to death on the kitchen floor."

Whitecastle's eyebrows drew together as he scratched his chest. "Bad?"

"It's a harmless nick." Wrenching her hand away from Max, she held it up in the air as evidence. A tiny drop of blood trickled down her wrist. She huffed, annoyed. "It's nothing."

"Then you'll be able to make it to the party?" Whitecastle asked.

She'd been half expecting the burly man to make an announcement that he had uncovered yet another bone. The invitation was a relief—and caught her by surprise. "What party?"

"The one I'm givin' tonight. Just a little spur-of-the-moment thing." He smiled a wide, toothy grin that seemed to sink into all three of his chins. "My boy Billy's finally decided to get married."

The honeymoon would undoubtedly be paid for by the money she'd spent having three separate foundations dug for a stable that had yet to be constructed, Rikki thought, then stopped. She'd skipped over the obvious. "You're inviting me?" It was her first invitation to a party in Senora.

"Yeah. Don't figure Max here'll come without you." Max shot him a look of reprimand. "'Course, you're welcome on your own, too, seeing as you're the doc," the older man added hastily. He began edging away, apparently aware that he was making matters worse. "Um, I'd better get back to work." He hiked his sagging pants up by the wide belt that secured them beneath his large belly and hurried out.

The invitation had been backhanded. Still, White-castle had made an observation that intrigued her. "Now what do you suppose gave him that idea?"

"Roger's sharper than he looks," Max answered casually. "Got any bandages?"

"He'd have to be." She looked at the man's wide back as he disappeared from view. "In the bathroom." She led the way.

He opened the medicine cabinet before she could. "You looked surprised when he invited you." He was afraid to take anything out, anticipating an avalanche from the three overflowing shelves if he did.

"I was. I've been here almost a year and no one's ever invited me to a party before." Holding her hand up to stop the flow of blood, she carefully moved things on the shelves with her free hand. "Except for a small trickle of business, I've always felt pretty much like an outsider, knocking on the door."

Max caught a roll of tape as it fell and placed it on the sink. "You don't strike me as the type to knock."

"No, not for long," she agreed. "Not when I'm not wanted."

"It's not that." He held back three vials of something green and liquid as Rikki extracted the box of bandages. "They're just a little slow in accepting new people. Once they do, you're part of them forever, no matter where you go."

She stopped. That sounded heavenly. "Like you?"

"Like me." He didn't think anything of it. He had never known another way. "That's why the sheriff called me when you found that bone."

"I didn't find it," she corrected. "Whitecastle did. Now, every time I see him, I keep waiting for him to tell me that he's discovered another one." She knew there was a bottle of Merthiolate here somewhere. Where was it?

"Well, he seems to be having as much luck at it lately as I have." Rikki turned to him, an alert look on her face. "None," he answered her glance.

Disappointment followed, though she tried to look on the bright side. "Which means I'll get my stable built."

"Among other things."

"Such as?"

"You might be rid of us soon." He watched her face to see her reaction.

The disappointment grew. "Oh?"

"I've only got a limited amount of funds to spend here. There might not be any more dinosaur bones to be found. I can't very well turn your whole property upside down looking."

Rikki saw the Merthiolate bottle next to the nail-polish remover she had yet to open. She eased it out. "No, you can't," she agreed quietly. *You've already turned my life upside down. That should be enough.*

"Here, let me." Max took the bottle from her and unscrewed the cap.

Rikki forced a smile to her lips. "Have you got this mad desire to coat things?"

He dabbed a little of the medication on the cut, then applied a little more. "Hmm?"

"I've watched you shellac those bones," she reminded him. She tried not to react as he blew on her finger to dry it.

"No, no mad desire to coat things." He took out a bandage, stripped off the wrapper and tossed it into the pail. "I reserve my mad desires for other things." He looked at her pointedly as he wrapped the bandage around her thumb.

"Like dinosaurs." It was only that, and not her, which would keep him here. Self-consciously, she took her hand away. "Nice surgery, Professor."

"Thanks. Yes." He stretched out the word as he looked at her. "Dinosaurs, too."

"Too?" She closed the box of bandages and maneuvered it back into place. The Merthiolate bottle was a little trickier. "I thought that was your main passion in life." Mission accomplished, she closed the medicine cabinet door and turned to face him.

"Funny, I thought the same thing, a little while ago," he said.

Rikki walked out of the bathroom ahead of him, not wanting him to see the smile on her lips. "How little?"

"A couple of weeks," he said offhandedly. "Maybe three. I lose track."

"Typical absentminded professor." She knew it was silly to hope he was serious. But she did.

He took her hand and swung her around. Surprised, Rikki fit right into the space created by his arms. "That's me, typical." Because he had craved the taste of her mouth, he gave himself up to the urge that had been battering his body all day.

He kissed her. Kissed her as if she was the first woman ever created. And she was, for him. Each time he kissed her, there was something new to uncover, another layer to strip away, from himself and from her. Kissing her released desire, white-hot and demanding, within him. It confused him. There was no logic, no rhyme or reason.

There didn't have to be.

There was only her.

His lips, warm, searching, roaming lightly over her face, undid her completely, as they had before. This time

she didn't fight it. She didn't want to. This was the stuff
memories were made of. This would be all she had once
he was gone. She absorbed each ray that shot through
her, memorized every movement of his hands as they slid
along her back, molding her to him.

Rikki rested her hands on his arms, once again needing to fill her lungs with air. Oxygen was at a premium
each time he kissed her. Slowly she shook her head, still
dizzy. "No, not so typical."

Max released her and held her at arm's length for a
moment. He studied her face, memorizing the curve of
her lips, the slope of her cheek. Everything. "I'll pick
you up at eight." He started to leave.

"Max?"

He stopped and turned around, his hand on the door.
"Yes?"

He was leaving without doing whatever it was he had
come in to do. "What did you come in for?"

The glow he felt inside gave way to a grin. "Can't you
guess?"

She shook her head, mystified.

"You."

No, not typical at all, she repeated to herself silently
as she watched him walk away through the screen door.
Elliot ran up to him as though he had been waiting for
Max to appear.

That made two of them, Rikki thought.

Chapter Nine

Dressing up had never been very important to her. That had always been her mother's domain. And Virginia's. Rikki enjoyed living her life in jeans and work shirts. But it was different tonight. This was going to be the first time that Max would see her in something that showed her legs. She wanted the first time to be special.

She stared into the closet at the clothes that had been part of another life, a life she had closed the door on. The clothes hanging before her had been too pretty to get rid of, but they had no place in the way she lived her life now.

Rikki chewed on her lower lip. She wanted to stand out and yet blend in. It wasn't an easy matter.

Finally she settled on doing something elaborate with her hair while keeping everything else simple. That settled, she found she had to hurry to get ready. The doorbell rang just as she was putting on her shoes.

"I'll get it," she called out, afraid that Virginia would beat her to the door and subject Max to another dose of unsubtle machinations aimed at bringing the two of them together in holy matrimony.

Not that that would be such a bad idea, Rikki mused. Just not coming from Virginia.

Hurrying down the stairs, Rikki reached the front door just ahead of Elliot. Virginia, mercifully, was nowhere to be seen.

"Wow." Elliot's eyes were round behind his large glasses.

She kissed the top of his head. "Thank you, I needed that." Ruffling his hair, she asked, "Since I can't play checkers with you tonight, what are you planning to do with yourself?"

"Oh, I'll find something." He grinned, and she wondered what he was up to, but just then Max ran the bell again.

She thought it was odd that he didn't stay around to talk to Max. In the past few weeks, the two of them had gotten very close. Elliot was hungry for a man's attention. Wallace never seemed to have enough time to spare for his son.

Rikki took a deep breath and opened the door. He was on her doorstep, wearing a blue dress shirt, open at the throat, and a pair of gray slacks. Very smooth, she thought.

When Max didn't say anything, she took it to mean that he didn't care for the outfit she was wearing. "I wasn't sure what to wear."

He watched her tug up the peasant blouse as it began to slide down one shoulder. The desire to stay her hand crossed his mind, but he pushed it back. "You made the right choice." His voice was deep, resonant, and she heard a note of underlying appreciation in it.

She looked down, smoothing the wide multicolored skirt. "You don't think it's too much?" Suddenly she felt like twirling around for him, holding out her skirt, but she checked the impulse. He would probably think she'd lost her mind, acting like a silly girl. But he made her want to act silly. To grab hold of every moment and enjoy it.

"Possibly not enough," he murmured, almost to himself. When she breathed, the low neckline moved, enticing him, creating thoughts that made his adrenaline rise to dangerous heights.

He *didn't* like it after all. She knew she should have worn the dress slacks and sweater top instead. "I can change." She turned to go.

"Don't you dare." He grabbed her wrist before she could get away. Rikki looked at him in surprise as pleasure from the sudden physical contact spilled through her. Max slid his hand from her wrist to her palm and entwined their fingers. "We'll be late. You don't want to get a reputation for being late, do you?"

She picked up her shawl and purse where she had left them on a nearby chair in the living room. "At least they'd notice me."

How could anyone help but notice her? "Oh, they've noticed you all right. And even if they hadn't before, they certainly will now."

He opened the door for her. Dusk was beginning to fall. There were moments when he thought that this was his favorite time of day. Everything seemed so peaceful. "We'll take my Land Rover, if that's all right with you."

She thought it was sweet of him to ask. "I don't mind. You probably know the way better in the dark than I do." She stopped on the porch and held out her shawl to him. A quizzical look rose in Max's eyes. "Would you mind?" she prompted.

Because she seemed to expect it, he took the shawl from her. "Mind what?"

"The shawl." She indicated it with her eyes, hiding an amused smile.

Max looked at it. It was white and lacy, with silver threads all through it. Feminine. It suited her. "It's very nice."

The smile turned into a grin. "It goes around my shoulders."

"Yes?" He looked at her blankly, then realized that she was waiting for him to put it around her. "Oh."

With movements that were far less fluid than he would have liked, Max slipped the shawl around her partially bare shoulders. His fingertips lightly brushed her skin. Desire tugged hard, bringing with it a need to pull away the blouse completely, to take Rikki in his arms and forget all about the party, the dinosaur and everything else, except for her.

He wondered if he was coming down with something. It was totally unlike him to want to push everything into the background this way. With a sigh, he slid the shawl into place. "You must think I'm a thick-headed clod."

She turned her head to look at him. "None of those words ever entered my head."

"What word did enter?"

It seemed right and natural for her to take his arm as they walked to his car. "Sweet."

"Oh, God," he groaned, "that sounds like you're describing a seven-year-old boy acting in his first school play." He pulled open the car door. Rikki tucked her wide skirt around her as she slid in.

"Speaking of little boys, is Elliot getting in your way?"

Max got in behind the wheel and pulled the seat belt around him. "No, as a matter of fact, he's being rather helpful." He turned the key and the vehicle came to life. "We had a long discussion about dinosaurs today. He knows a lot."

She watched the way the headlights cut through the dark as they drove, ebbing and flowing on the ground like pools of water.

Darkness came fast out in the country, Max thought. After living in L.A. for nine months, with its artificial lights that kept night at bay, it was nice to get back to a rural area.

He smiled to himself. You can take the boy out of the country, but apparently it really wasn't easy taking the country out of the boy, he mused. "Yesterday I had him assisting one of the students with putting a cast on the last bone we uncovered."

Rikki turned to look at him. It sounded like an odd thing to do. "Why would you do that?"

He slowed as he searched for the turn that would take him to Whitecastle's place. "Well, I thought Elliot would—"

"No, I'm glad for anything you can do with Elliot. He loves this. I meant the cast. Why would you put a cast on a dinosaur bone? It's not as if you're trying to mend it." She stopped. There was a lot she didn't know about his field. "Are you?"

"No." He knew her well enough not to laugh and hurt her feelings, although she was adorable. Adorable. When had he ever applied that word to anything, let alone a woman? She made him see things differently. *Feel* differently. Just being with her was a revelation. "It preserves the larger ones for shipping back to the museum."

She tried to picture being surrounded by boxes containing dinosaur fossils. Boxes that had to be opened and sorted. "I sure wouldn't want to be there to unpack all those things."

"I would." He remembered the pleasure in being confronted with the task. It was always an exhilarating challenge. "It's like trying to solve a giant jigsaw puzzle, looking for the right bones to fit together. Sometimes we have to make an artificial one, so the skeleton will hold together."

When he talked about his work, he seemed like a child at Christmas. How could she hope to compete with that?

"Oh, I wasn't talking about the challenge. I'm sure that's really very exciting for you." She flashed a smile, not wanting him to think that she was denigrating the nature of his work. "I just hate unpacking with a passion. It seemed I was always packing and unpacking when I was a child."

He saw the slightest bit of tension tighten her jaw. It hadn't been there before. "Just how much *did* you travel around?"

Rikki frowned as she remembered those years. "Too much."

As a boy he had ached to travel somewhere farther than the fields that surrounded Senora. He had lain awake at night and dreamed of mysterious, faraway places where dinosaur bones lay buried, waiting for him to uncover them.

"I bet you saw an awful lot of interesting things, though."

"Oh, I did." There was no denying that. She had seen everything the tour books had thought was important. "The pyramids in Egypt, the Colosseum in Rome, Piccadilly Circus in London." She rolled the names off her tongue. "It would have made a wonderful vacation. But it made for a terrible way of life."

He tried to picture what there was not to like about it and failed. "Your parents certainly saw to it that you took in the sights."

He still didn't get it, she thought. It might have been nice, yes, if they had done all those things as a family. But they hadn't. Not once. "It wasn't their idea. It was my governess's. My parents were too busy being socialites." She saw the way he was looking at her and realized how that must have come across. "I'm sorry. That probably sounded awfully bitter to you."

His smile was understanding. "I think a better word is 'hurt.' "

She studied him for a moment. He had surprised her. "You know, for someone who can't take a hint about a shawl, you're awfully perceptive where it counts."

He laughed out loud.

"What's the joke?"

Max shook his head. "Nothing. I was just thinking of someone who might have argued with you about your evaluation."

"Your fiancée." Rikki wasn't asking. She knew. Without realizing it, she pulled the shawl tighter around her shoulders.

Max noticed that she had gone rigid and wondered why. "Yes."

She tried to remember what he had told her about his fiancée. There wasn't much to go on. "You said she was from around here." Max nodded in answer as he took a turn down another long, dark road. Rikki plunged ahead. "Will she be there tonight?" She hoped he didn't think she was being jealous. She wasn't. Well, not exactly, she amended.

"I don't see how." The headlights illuminated the long gravel driveway that led to the ranch house. "Last I heard, she was aspiring to the kind of life you hated."

"That would have given her something in common with you—travel." So why hadn't they gotten married?

He shook his head at her conclusion. "She wanted bright lights. New York. San Francisco. I'm not interested in seeing places like that. Just dinosaurs."

But you can't live by dinosaurs alone, she thought. Didn't he want more? "What about reality? What about life?"

He wondered at the urgent note in her voice. Did it really matter to her what he wanted? "Life's what you make it."

It sounded like such a simple philosophy. Maybe he was happy just the way he was. Which left no room for her and what she needed. Roots. "And what have you made yours into?"

Whitecastle's ranch house came into view. Max carefully guided the car toward an available space. "More or less what I've wanted. I've studied something that always fascinated me. Then taught it. I've been on some successful digs. I've got no regrets." He pulled up the hand brake and shut off the engine.

Well, no, maybe that was wrong, Max amended silently as he looked into her eyes. The lights from Whitecastle's house were bright, illuminating the interior of the car. Rikki's eyes were warm, stirring. Maybe he did have one regret. He would have liked to have had someone to share it all with. *Really* share. But life, he knew, wasn't fair, and sacrifices had to be made.

Wasn't that what he had told himself when Sally had left, leaving his self-esteem in tatters?

Looking at him, Rikki decided it was more or less what she surmised. He was content just the way he was. And all this, the blood-stirring kisses, the mind-fogging embraces, they were just a passing episode in his life. She had to keep that in mind. She could enjoy, but not too much. She could even love, but not too much.

Love? No, that couldn't enter the picture. She wouldn't allow it to happen. Because then she knew she wouldn't be able to keep things under control.

She wondered, as she took the hand he offered her and stepped out of the car, if she could keep anything under control, no matter what she told herself.

"Hey, Max, is that you?"

Max turned at the sound of the booming, exuberant voice. A tall, heavyset man with a full, neatly trimmed black beard agilely strode down the steps of the front porch to greet them.

"Allen?" Max let his hand be pumped up and down enthusiastically as he stared at the man before him.

The genial giant actually dwarfed Max as he clapped him on the back. "None other."

How long had it been? Too long, Max decided. "When did you get in?"

"Last night," Allen replied. Although he spoke to Max, he didn't try to hide the fact that he obviously appreciated the figure he saw standing next to his childhood friend. "Been visiting Dad. I brought down the whole tribe." Allen turned to Max again. "He told me you were back, pawing the dirt, looking for that dinosaur of yours."

From the way the other man spoke, Rikki surmised that "finding his dinosaur" was something Max had set his heart on when he was a boy. Just as she had set her heart on having a home and roots. She tried to stave off the hopeless feeling that thought generated.

Allen looked past Max, flashing a broad, perfect smile at Rikki. "Seems that's not the only thing you found. You must be the new vet."

Rikki put out her hand and watched it being swallowed up by both of Allen's. "Must be. And you're..." She looked at Max for an explanation.

He put a proprietary hand on Rikki's shoulder. The gesture wasn't wasted on Allen. The wide grin grew impossibly large, like the man. "Allen Beamish, the sheriff's son." Allen's handshake was as hearty as he seemed to be.

"Erikka McGuire," Rikki told him. "But you already knew that."

"Yup." He gave her a long, purely male look and nodded approvingly. "But I don't know anything else." His brown eyes shone. He had the look of a frisky lion cub waiting to be played with.

"As you must have guessed," Max said, guiding Rikki toward the porch steps, "Allen is the shy, retiring type. And if I let him, he'll keep us out here all night, just talking."

Rikki could think of worse things than spending the evening listening to stories from a man who had known Max intimately as a boy.

Allen threw back his head and laughed. The image of a lion cub was sustained. A large, clumsy, lovable lion cub. Allen took Rikki's arm and ushered her toward the house, pushing open the front door. "I can hear the band starting up. I get the first dance,'' he informed Rikki.

Very firmly, Max drew Rikki away from his friend. "You get the *next* dance. Maybe," Max threw over his shoulder as he took Rikki into his arms.

She liked the fact that he was acting protectively toward her. A warm glow rose within her. As he turned her around on the floor, Rikki noticed their host. "Shouldn't we say hello to Mr. Whitecastle first?"

"Hellos aren't necessary around here. He sees us." Max nodded at the white-haired man standing in a cluster of older men.

Dancing seemed to come effortlessly to Max. Another surprise. "You dance rather well for a scholar."

Her smile warmed him. "You have to do something while you're on a dig."

"Did Julia teach you?" She kept her tone intentionally light, but she doubted if she fooled him. She could see him dancing with Julia, holding her close, the way he was holding her now. Rikki had no business whatsoever feeling the small, sharp prick of jealousy. She knew that. But it was there anyway.

Max entwined his fingers through hers, his other hand once again pressing the small of her back. "Nope. Ivan did."

"Ivan?"

Max nodded, remembering. "Short, gnarled old man who talked out of one side of his mouth and looked as if he belonged in an old movie. But he moved like Fred Astaire. He was our guide in Central America." The scene came back to him. "One of the archaeologists had some old tapes and a cassette player with him. One evening, after it had rained for three days straight, Ivan offered to teach me how to dance. I guess he could only take so much boredom.''

"Ivan would have been proud," Rikki murmured. She rested her cheek against his chest, feeling oddly secure, yet aroused at the same time. This man, she decided, was full of surprises. She raised her head to look up at him. "So would Fred."

He smiled at her. For a moment he just absorbed the warmth he felt, holding her. The light scent of her perfume wafted into his senses. It made him think of springtime. That had always been his favorite time of year. Springtime. A time for rebirth. A time for promises to be made and possibly fulfilled. But that was for later. Spring was for hope.

He wondered where he would be next spring and discovered that he didn't want to think about that, about leaving here. Leaving Rikki. It was a new experience for him. He had always thought about leaving, about the next dig, the next challenge, even while work was progressing on the one where he was.

Always. Until now.

Allen tapped him on the shoulder. Max spared him a single glance. "Later." With that, he guided Rikki's steps away from the burly man.

Rikki laughed as they left Allen standing there, shaking his head and grinning. "That wasn't very polite."

"Allen and I don't have to be polite. We're friends."

"Must be nice."

He peered down at her face, wondering what she had been like as a child. What her life had really been like. "Don't you have any friends?"

"Acquaintances," Rikki corrected. "Lots of acquaintances." She thought for a moment. "My best friend was an old woman who wore sensible shoes and taught me how to conjugate Latin verbs."

He thought that a little odd and yet endearing. "Have you seen her lately?"

Rikki shook her head. She found it still hurt to think about Edith. "She died a year ago. I didn't go to the funeral. I didn't want to say goodbye." She pressed her lips together. "I hate that word." She realized she had spoken with a little too much feeling. "Sorry."

How would she look when it came time for him to say goodbye? he wondered. He didn't want to know.

"How's our foal doing?" he asked softly, instinctively knowing that she needed to think about something that embodied the promise of life.

She liked the fact that he referred to the colt as theirs. She knew it was foolish, but she let herself indulge in the feeling for a moment. "Getting stronger by the day. Mama's doing just fine, too." Her pleasure was evident in her eyes.

He wanted to kiss her, to sweep her away from the crowd and make love to her. "Mama had a good doctor."

She didn't take compliments very well. She never had. Maybe because she had heard so many of them when she was growing up, all ringing false. The people who populated her parents' circle of friends always said things they didn't mean.

"I did what had to be done. It's what I was trained to do." She looked at him. The music had stopped, but she didn't want to. She wanted to go on dancing. With Max. Reluctantly she let her hand drop. "How's the dig going?"

"It's going," he said evasively.

"Anything new?" she pressed hopefully. "Or old?"

Max smiled at her correction. "No to both." There was no point in lying to her. "Seems my dinosaur kept himself together more than I would have wanted him to. At least, he didn't seem to let any more of himself end up here."

Rikki suddenly had a mental picture of a dinosaur hobbling around, holding on to limbs that were about to fall off.

"What kind do you think it was, or is it too soon to tell?" She nodded at someone she recognized and was pleased that the man responded with a genial smile.

Max drew her over to a small table where there was a large punch bowl filled with ruby-colored liquid. "Roger's own brand of wine," Max explained. He proceeded to fill two glasses. "Going by the level where we found the first bone and what was prevalent in this section of the country, my guess is that it was a *Labocania*." He handed her a glass.

Rikki took it in both hands. "Not an *Apatosaurus?*" She watched his face to see if she had gotten the pronunciation right.

He grinned. "Not unless he lost his way. They're usually found around the upper Midwest."

"Maybe he was visiting." She took a tentative sip of the wine. Her eyes watered slightly as she looked up at Max in wonder.

"It does have a kick," he agreed, though the sip he took had no visible effect on him.

The man had a cast-iron stomach, she thought. But then, he drank that coffee of his on a daily basis. "I never heard of a *Labocania* before."

"The name derives from the La Bocana Roja rock formation in Baja California. He had a massive skull and looked a little like a *Tyrannosaurus,* except smaller and stockier." Max watched her set aside her glass discreetly. He set his own down next to it. Being with her was intoxicating enough without the benefit of any wine.

He smiled as he took her hand. The music was beginning again. "Ask Elliot. He knows a lot about it. He's very bright."

"And I'm very grateful that you've been so nice to him." Warm sensations spread over her as she felt his arms around her.

"Hard not to." The music had a quick beat, but he preferred moving slowly. He liked her body pressed against him no matter what the tempo. "He reminds me of me at that age. Too studious for my own good."

"Everybody's got to have a fault."

"And Max's is that he hogs all the good things he finds. My turn." Allen squeezed in between them, not an easy trick considering his girth, Rikki thought, amused. "Doris wants her turn at you."

"Doris?" She tried to sound nonchalant but suspected that she had failed when she saw the smallest glimmer of a smile on Max's lips.

"My wife," Allen clarified, taking Rikki into his bearlike hold. "You're good for my friend," he told her. He saw the slight flush enter her cheeks. "Hey, now, I'm not the reserved type. That's for Max. Except he doesn't seem to be, around you." Allen winked secretively. "I've been watching."

"I suppose there's no use denying it or arguing with you."

"None whatsoever."

She thought of the stubborn set of the sheriff's jaw when he had told her that she couldn't go on digging until he called in the proper authority to examine the bone. "You're like your father."

Allen's grin emerged from beneath his beard, filling out his broad cheeks even farther. "Taught him everything he knows," Allen assured her as he whirled her around on the floor.

Whitecastle nodded at the couple approvingly as Rikki sped by. "Glad you could make it."

"So am I," she answered wholeheartedly.

Chapter Ten

He had forgotten how much fun he could have in the company of old friends. The years had melted away for Max, and it was almost as if he'd never left the warm homes and hearths of Senora. Now, driving back to Rikki's house, things settled into place. Time had passed for all of them, of course. His father was gone. Allen was fifty pounds heavier and had a family. And he had gotten to a place in his life he had always aspired to.

Or thought he had.

Driving slowly, Max turned his head and smiled. Everything seemed to fade in the presence of the petite woman sitting next to him. "Don't look now, but you're glowing."

So it showed. "I had a very good time." The best she could recall.

The feeling of contentment was infectious. He wanted to slip one arm around her shoulders. A Land Rover, though, was not constructed to encourage romance. He left both hands on the wheel. "Is that a compliment?"

She would have accused someone else of being coy. But not Max. "Partially."

"Which part?"

Word games were something she had gladly left behind her when she had abandoned her parents' life-style. With Max, there could only be the truth. "The part that enjoyed dancing with you and talking to you—and having you introduce me to everyone."

He detected a sense of satisfaction, perhaps even pleasure, in her voice. "Fitting in means a lot to you, doesn't it?"

"Yes." She wasn't used to being so open. It was so easy to talk to him, to admit things. Who would she talk to when he was gone?

No, she wasn't going to spoil the evening. Logic was something for tomorrow, not for a perfect night like tonight.

Fitting in had never been important to him. But then, he'd never had to try, either. He just always had, in his own way, on his own terms. There had always been people around who knew him and cared. Wherever he went, there was always someone who greeted him, inquiring about how he was doing. It was something he just took for granted.

"Funny, you didn't seem like the type who would care that much about fitting in. You seemed to be so independent, digging posts, doing whatever needed to be done." He grinned, remembering. "Getting dirty."

She thought of yesterday, when he had run into her just as she was getting back to the house. She'd been working all morning repairing a section of fence. There wasn't a single part of her that hadn't had dust on it.

She'd felt like something the cat had dragged in, an assessment that Virginia had quickly seconded. "I do that a lot. Get dirty, I mean."

"I like your spirit, Rikki. Your independence." It showed that she wasn't afraid to do what needed to be done. Even though she needed to belong, she was still self-sufficient, still strong. There were a lot of similarities between them, he thought. The differences came in the way they had been raised.

"That's not all there is, Max."

"No." He glanced down at her blouse. The small tie had almost come undone. Temptation everywhere he turned, he thought. "There's a lot more than that to you."

She wanted to make him understand, to make him see. "I need roots, Max. I can do anything, as long as I know I belong somewhere."

Strange how they always seemed to come back to the one thing that made them so different. "We all belong somewhere, but it doesn't have to be a permanent thing."

"With me it does," she told him quietly, wishing it was the same for him. But it wasn't, and that was something she had to accept. Why couldn't she just enjoy now without looking to tomorrow? But she couldn't, no more than Max could stop looking for traces of yesterday.

"I see." He stared straight ahead as they drove up to the small, comfortable-looking house. There was a large red Mercedes parked directly in front of the porch. He gave Rikki a questioning look. It was rather late for visitors. "Expecting company?"

"No, I—" She stopped. A door slammed from within the house just as Rikki recognized the car. "That belongs to Wallace. My brother-in-law." And, from the sound of the slamming door, it looked as if the proverbial fat was hitting the fire.

"Virginia's husband?"

Rikki nodded as she got out of the Land Rover. Max followed suit and came around the front of the Mercedes. He whistled softly in appreciation. The car, except for some streaks of dust, was immaculate. He knew a lot of people who would have loved to own a car like that. To Max it was just a beautiful piece of workmanship, nothing more.

He had a feeling that Rikki might need him. It was nothing he could quite put his finger on, just instinct. But instinct had always served him well.

"If you don't mind, I'd like to stick around and meet him."

She looked at Max and smiled. No matter where his work had taken him, he still sounded like a hometown boy, polite to the nth degree, giving off an air of protectiveness. "Mind?" She winced as something crashed inside the house. "I have a feeling I'm going to need all the help I can get."

Max walked in front of her to the porch. "Is he short-tempered?"

The word for Wallace, if anything, was bland. "No, but Ginny is. Short-tempered, shortsighted and a little blind when it comes to understanding others."

So far there was absolutely no family resemblance between the two sisters, he thought. "Sounds like a wonderful gal."

There were good points to Virginia. They just didn't surface very often. "She is, when she's off in the right direction."

It wasn't always the oldest who was the steadfast one, he thought with a smile. "And it's up to you to send her there, right?"

"Something like that."

She took a deep breath, bracing herself for what lay ahead. Max took her hand in his, threaded his fingers through hers and squeezed lightly. It was just a small gesture of support, but it meant the world to her. She had never been supported before. With all the windmills she had tilted at, whether that involved going to veterinary school or just choosing her own clothes, she had always been met with strong opposition. She had had to face everything alone. Two was a very nice number, she thought.

"'Into the valley of death rode the six hundred,'" Rikki murmured under her breath as she unlocked the front door.

Max laughed as she deposited the key in her purse. "Is it going to be as bad as all that?"

"Trust me, it will be an experience." She pushed open the door. A book went flying by not a foot away, and she jerked back, pulling the door closed again. "Any more questions?" She looked over her shoulder at Max.

He wasn't used to such visual displays of emotion. "I take it you're the even-tempered one in the family."

"Compared to her I am."

"Thanks for the warning."

She had let Virginia stay with her, nursing, as far as Rikki was concerned, imaginary wounds, but this was really going too far. She wasn't about to have her home reduced to a battleground. Rikki pushed open the door again. "Virginia, we're coming in!"

The room was empty. And obviously much the worse for wear.

"Looks like war broke out and we made it in for the last volley." Max picked up the coatrack from the floor and righted it.

Rikki retrieved a wide-brimmed Stetson she was very fond of and hung it back on the rack. "Don't count on it." Max heard the restrained temper simmering in her voice. "Elliot?" she called, looking around. He was her main concern right now. But there was no answer from her nephew. Miraculously, he seemed to be sleeping through all this.

Instead, Virginia, wearing a scarlet peignoir, burst in with a vengeance through the dining room door on the left. "How *could* you?"

Rikki picked up two of the sofa cushions from the floor and threw them into place a little too vigorously. "I'm not sure. How could I what?" She looked around at the wreckage and drew a sharp breath. She knew that Virginia wasn't used to thinking of other people's property as not belonging to her, but there was only so much leeway she could allow her sister. Magazines, books and bric-a-brac were scattered everywhere, a testimony to Virginia's anger.

Max saw her expression and was glad that he had never been on the receiving end of Rikki's wrath. It would not, he thought, be a pretty thing. For the time being, he thought it prudent to keep out of this.

Virginia's scarlet-nailed hand clutched at one of the few remaining pillows on the sofa, pulling it to her. "Wallace said you called him. *How could you call him?*"

Rikki pulled the pillow away from her sister's grasp, her eyes on Virginia's face, daring her to take it back. Virginia dropped her hand. "I thought you wanted him to come after you."

Virginia looked around for something to release her anger on. Max moved casually to the right and blocked her path to the television set. He smiled at her, and she tossed her head. "I did."

"He couldn't do that if he didn't know where you were." Logic, Rikki knew, was wasted on Virginia. The genes that carried their father's steel-trap mind had been on vacation the night Virginia had been conceived.

Virginia whirled on her. "If he cared, he would have found out."

She began to pick up an end table. Max silently righted its mate. "He did find out," Rikki pointed out.

Virginia threw up her hands in exasperation. "I meant through a detective or something."

Enough was enough. "For God's sake, Virginia, what does it matter how he found out? He's here. Make up," she snapped. "And then lend me a hand in cleaning all this up." She gestured about the room.

A tall, scholarly man, drawn by the sound of a rational voice, walked into the room looking ill at ease. Max could immediately see where Elliot had gotten his features.

Wallace Claremont flashed Rikki an embarrassed smile. "Hello, Erikka."

"Hi, Wallace." Tossing the book she had picked up from the floor onto the sofa, Rikki gave him a quick hug. "I see the war's not going very well."

The camaraderie between her sister and her husband obviously annoyed Virginia, Max noted. Virginia was undoubtedly used to being the center of attention.

"How can you joke?" Virginia demanded.

Rikki swung around to look at her. "Because if I don't joke, I might just wrap my hands around your lovely throat."

"I see what you mean about being the calm one only in comparison," Max interjected.

Wallace seemed to notice him for the first time, a question rising in his eyes before they darted back to Virginia.

Max might not have been on the front lines of many relationships, but he knew suspicion when he saw it. "David Maxwell." He put out his hand to Wallace, and the other man took it. The handshake was a little limp as Wallace continued to regard Max with suspicion. "I'm conducting an archaeological dig on Rikki's property." The look on Wallace's face remained. "I'm with *her*." With a grin, he pointed to Rikki.

"Oh." Wallace's furrowed brow smoothed out.

The uncomfortable moment of suspicion and jealousy passed, the round somehow going to Virginia. "How does it feel?" Virginia thrust her face forward.

"Terrible," Wallace admitted. Bright myopic blue eyes looked at the woman who had been his wife for fourteen years. "Everything's terrible without you."

Virginia had trouble hiding her triumphant smile. It was the first time in three weeks that Rikki had seen her look so content. "You should have thought of that before you started spending time with Janine."

"Janet," Wallace corrected automatically.

Virginia's triumph wavered as her perfectly arched brows rose. "You have two of them?"

Wallace threw up his hands. "I don't even have one of them." He looked to Rikki for help, but she raised her hands, palms out. She had done as much as she was going to. Wallace turned to face Virginia. "Janet's my secretary's name, not Janine. Or was." His voice rose, with only a slight temper. "You don't have the name straight or the situation."

But Virginia had caught the word she wanted. "What do you mean, was?"

"I fired her."

A smile began to form, but she wasn't totally convinced yet. "And set her up in a penthouse."

Wallace, Max thought, had the look of a man at the end of his rope. If *he* had been married to Virginia, he would have used that rope to hang himself. Max looked at Rikki with renewed appreciation.

"I don't know where she's living, Virginia." Wallace reached for her hand, only to have Virginia move away. "I don't care. I just want you and Elliot home again."

Rikki watched her sister move around the room. The fury and frustration were gone. She knew she'd won. Virginia was now toying with Wallace. Rikki bit back the temptation to intervene. Wallace, when he got home, would be within his rights to give Virginia a good tongue-lashing. She knew she wanted to.

"A likely story," Virginia sniffed.

Wallace spread his hands in supplication. "It's the *only* story."

"Then why didn't you try to find me?"

"Because I wanted you to cool off. I didn't think you'd listen to reason while you were so angry."

Rikki couldn't hold back any longer. "I have news for you, Wallace. She doesn't listen to it very much when she's *not* angry, either."

Virginia looked at Rikki haughtily, obviously miffed at having her drama interrupted. "I don't have to stay here and take this abuse."

It was time to wrap this up. Virginia looked as if she was going for an epic. "No," Rikki agreed heartily, "you don't." She placed her hands on her sister's shoulders and turned her toward Wallace. "You have a nice house with a nice husband and a terrific kid to go back to." She gave Virginia a little shove, pushing her into a surprised Wallace's arms. "I suggest you take advantage of all that niceness and leave."

Virginia's eyes opened wide in shock. "It's the middle of the night."

Rikki looked at her watch pointedly. "Dawn is only five hours away."

"Four," Max corrected.

"Four," Rikki echoed, nodding at Max. She drew a breath, then relinquished it. "All right, you can stay until then, provided that you two sleep in the same bed while you wait."

Virginia raised her chin, crossing her arms in front of her. "You can't order me around."

This time Rikki refused to be provoked. As far as she was concerned, she held all the cards. "It's my house, I can order anyone around I want." She looked from Wallace to Max. "Right, fellas?"

"Absolutely," Max said. "Territorial rights come first." He winked at Rikki.

"She's got you there, Virginia." A smile began to lift the corners of Wallace's thin lips.

Virginia huffed. She knew when she had lost. "All right. I can't wait to leave this godforsaken place, anyway." She turned, one scarlet satin heel digging into the polished wood floor. "The room's upstairs. But you stay on your own side of the bed," she warned with royal haughtiness as she climbed up the stairs.

Wallace grinned his thanks to Rikki, then followed his wife.

Rikki let out a long breath, relieved. The house would be still soon. And hers again. "I give them half an hour. Wallace can be very persuasive in bed." She turned her attention to picking up the magazines that were scattered around the floor.

Max joined her, though his interest was in her comment. "How would you know?"

"Virginia told me." She stacked the magazines on the coffee table, lining up the edges neatly. That done, she paused and looked at Max. "Very little is sacred to her, especially when she's trying to convince someone of something."

Max retrieved the cut-glass bowl from beneath the table and placed it in the center. "What was she trying to convince you to do?"

The candy she kept in the bowl for Elliot was scattered everywhere. Rikki got on her knees and began gathering the cellophane-wrapped sour balls. "Get married."

Their hands met over an orange sour ball. "To anyone in particular?"

Rikki deposited the handful she'd scooped up into the bowl. A grin played on her lips. So, he was interested. Maybe there *was* hope. "A man."

That didn't sound right to him. He could see Virginia trying to arrange something that would reflect well on her, not just any match. Maybe she wasn't as self-absorbed as he thought. "Nothing more specific?"

"No, just a man." Rikki reached under the sofa and snared three more sour balls of different colors. "Any man." She crawled back out, unaware that Max had stopped and taken a very vested interest in the way her posterior moved as she went sour ball hunting. "She says I have an obligation to carry on the family heritage." The sour balls clinked against the glass as they joined the others. "She sounds a lot like my parents used to, before they gave up on me."

There was something seductive about the way the light played over her face. If there was a battle to be fought against temptation, he thought, he was losing it. "They shouldn't have. Looks to me as if they missed out on something pretty terrific."

Rikki sat back on her heels, her hand raised over the bowl with another deposit. "You know, for a man who's only interested in dinosaurs, you say some pretty nice things."

His smile was warm and only for her. "Yes, I do, don't I?"

Rikki grinned. "Modest, too."

"No," he admitted honestly, "stunned."

Rikki shook her head. "You've lost me."

That, he thought, was what he was afraid of. When it came time for him to go, she would stay. It was something he didn't want to think about right now, but something that would have to be considered later. Very carefully. "I never used to say the right thing."

Rikki frowned. "Is that something else Sally told you?" Sally and Virginia, Rikki was beginning to think, were two of a kind.

"Yes, but she was right. She told me I had a better relationship with my tools than I did with her." And when he thought about it later, after she had left, he had realized that he probably did.

Rikki didn't like Max saying disparaging things about himself. "Maybe she just wasn't the right woman for you."

"No, she wasn't." And he knew now who was. But there were a lot of other factors that were going to have to be ironed out first. And perhaps a lot of convincing to be done, as well.

Every journey, he told himself, began with the first step. Max lowered his mouth to hers and kissed her.

It was a soft kiss, with more than a hint of recklessness waiting just beyond. For both of them. He had held her in his arms and touched her all evening without being able to give way to the tide of desire that had been churning inside him. He'd been a predictable, uncomplicated, calm man all his life. She'd changed that. She had thrown all his predictability out the window. Emotions like the ones he was now experiencing weren't supposed to take center stage; they weren't supposed to threaten to rule him.

And yet he didn't care.

It was as simple as that. He would trade all the peace and predictability in the world in order to have her in his arms. In order to kiss her. To share this magic, whatever it was that made magic, with her.

This was something totally new for him. For the first time in his life, he was questioning his wandering way of life. Here, he thought, was a very nice place to be.

He felt his heart pounding in his ears. "This is getting to be very habit-forming."

"Tell me about it." She laughed against his lips. And then the laughter moved inside, spreading sunshine in the wake of passion, making it all swirl together until it consumed her entirely. She was drowning, and she didn't care. Her body leaned into his, and they continued the dance they had shared in Whitecastle's house but without moving an inch. This time it was a dance of their souls, a timeless ritual that could end only one way.

When he kissed her like that, she forgot about their differences, but they were all there, waiting for her, as soon as he stopped.

Rikki braced her hands against his chest and pushed, though not hard. In another second she was going to be lost. "You have work to do tomorrow," she said breathlessly when he drew his lips from hers.

She was his for the taking. He could feel it. It made pulling back that much harder. But he had to. Until he thought things through, it wouldn't be fair to her to play upon a moment of vulnerability. "Actually, I have work to do tonight." And he would never get to it if he stayed here for another moment. His restraint was worn almost clean through.

"Max, I—"

"Shh." He rose to his feet and took her hand, bringing her up with him. "Don't say anything either one of us is going to regret. Mostly me." He dropped a kiss on her temple. "I'll see you in the morning."

She watched him go, aching to make him stay, knowing that this was the right thing to do and that she should be grateful to him for being stronger than she was.

There were times when Rikki absolutely hated doing the right thing.

The commotion of chairs being moved away from the kitchen table made Rikki turn around. It was hard to believe these were the same two combatants who had fought in her living room only a few hours ago.

"I see you two have made up." She set the stack of pancakes on the table before Wallace and Virginia.

Virginia placed her hand over her husband's. "Wallace and I did a lot of talking last night."

Rikki turned back to the stove before her grin gave her away. Wallace and Virginia had certainly done a lot of something last night, but she had a feeling it wasn't talking. There was too much of a glow to Virginia this morning to be explained by mere words. No, that could only come when you loved someone. As flighty and un-centered as Virginia was, Rikki envied her that. Envied her the contentment that came from finding the right man, loving the right man.

But it wasn't that simple, really. Finding and keeping were two different things. Finding involved luck. Keeping involved reality. And reality had a way of ruining more things than it enhanced.

She ought to know.

Rikki turned around just as Max walked in. His eyes were still sleepy, and he had the rumpled look that getting only a few hours of sleep achieved. Since they had all gotten to bed so late, Rikki had postponed breakfast until seven, but sleep hadn't come easily, not for her. She wondered if he had been up, thinking, the way she had. She had reached some important conclusions. Conclusions to be shared with him once she got Virginia and Wallace on their way. Elliot would stay for the summer. But Elliot had never been any trouble.

She smiled warmly as she placed a second stack of pancakes on the table, this time in front of Max. Sleepy or not, the man could eat up a storm. She'd learned that about him. Learned a lot in a very short time.

"Where's Elliot?" she asked her sister, looking at his empty place.

Virginia stared at it as if she expected him to materialize. "I thought he'd be down here, with you."

When she left, Rikki was going to miss Virginia. In about a year or so. "Well, he's not."

"I'll go get him," Wallace volunteered, getting up. "Which is his room?"

"First room on the right at the head of the stairs." It was odd for Elliot to be sleeping in. It wasn't like him.

Now that she thought about it, it hadn't been like him not to come down when Virginia and Wallace were having their "discussion" in the living room. Elliot wasn't the type to cower. He would have been there, trying to solve things. Why hadn't he? Could he really have slept that soundly?

Instinct told her that something was wrong before Wallace reentered the kitchen. He was holding a note in his hand, a somber expression on his face. Rikki wiped her hands on her apron as she crossed to him. Without waiting to ask, she took the note from him.

"He says he's going to go after his own dinosaur and that we shouldn't worry." She stared at the note. There was more. Elliot thought that if he found one, his parents would both be proud of him and stop fighting with each other. He had obviously misunderstood what the argument had been about. She raised her eyes to look at Wallace, who couldn't meet her gaze.

Max was on his feet, looking over her shoulder at the precise writing. Rikki turned to him, telling herself not to overreact. "Do you know where he could have gone?"

Max shook his head. He didn't like this. Elliot had no business wandering off by himself. "No. We talked about the different places dinosaurs could be found yesterday. I mentioned that the best find I ever had was in a cave."

"There's a cave on my property. I took him there last summer on a picnic." Rikki crumpled the note and let it fall to the table, a shiver of fear snaking up her spine.

Chapter Eleven

"He's not in any danger, is he?" There was concern etched on Wallace's face as he looked at Rikki.

"No," she lied.

She wanted to shout, "Of course he's in danger. He's a little boy, wandering around in a cave by himself," but shouting would serve no purpose. It would only make things worse. Virginia would become hysterical, and Rikki was *not* up to dealing with that.

"Elliot's sensible." Rikki glanced at the crumpled note on the table. "At least, I thought he was before he wrote that." She forced a smile for Wallace and Virginia's sake. "But when I find him, I'm going to tan his hide for not telling me where he was going." She took off her apron and threw it on the back of Elliot's empty chair.

She wasn't fooling Max. He knew her well enough to know the signs. "I'm going with you."

She had done things alone for so long, she wasn't used to asking for help. Or getting it. Max saw gratitude rise in her eyes. "Don't you have a dinosaur to find?" she asked.

He shrugged off her question. "It's not going anywhere."

Wallace took hold of Rikki's arm. "What do you want me to do?"

Why did it always take some kind of a crisis to make some parents notice their children? Rikki wondered. "Hold on to your wife and stick around here in case our budding paleontologist returns while we're out looking for him."

Rikki shoved the swing door open with the flat of her hand, hurrying to the front door. Max was right behind her. The false smile left her lips. She stopped short when she saw Diego through the living room window. He was leading one of her horses.

"That's Silky, the horse Elliot rides." Rikki ran to the front door and pulled it open. She descended the porch steps two at a time, telling herself that she was getting excited for no reason. It didn't help. "Diego, where are you taking Silky?"

The sun-darkened face was somber. "Señorita Rikki, I find him wandering around by himself just now." Diego glanced over his shoulder, as if Elliot was going to appear there. "But I do not see your nephew. Is he going for a ride?"

Without thinking, she linked her fingers with Max's, gathering his strength to her. "He's already gone."

"But I do not understa—"

She didn't have time to explain. "When did you get to the stables this morning?" Rikki interrupted.

Diego shrugged, thinking. "Sometime around five. Maybe five-fifteen. Why? Is the boy missing?"

"Yes," Rikki answered grimly.

Why would he do something so stupid? This wasn't like him. Rikki looked up at Max. "Damn, why didn't I check on him before I went to bed? I could have talked to him. He wouldn't have gone if he'd had someone to make him feel that everything was going to be all right."

"You had no way of knowing what was on his mind, Rikki." Max could see that he wasn't easing her conscience. "The horse might just have run off by itself if it wasn't tethered properly." He grew stern, hoping to snap her out of the panic he saw growing in her eyes. "This doesn't necessarily mean he's hurt."

"No, but the longer he stays out there, the more likely it is that he *will* get hurt. He's smart, but he's not very good in the outdoors, camping, hiking, things like that." The panic that had been steadily growing in the pit of her stomach refused to let go. She hurried into the stable.

Max followed. "Don't you think it would be a better idea to take the Land Rover?" he asked, just as she picked up a saddle.

Rikki stopped. He was right. She wasn't thinking clearly. She had to get hold of herself. She wasn't going to do Elliot any good if she fell to pieces and let her imagination run away with her. "Okay, you're right. We'll drive." She dropped the saddle back on the bench and hurried out again.

Max grabbed her hand. "Rikki, take it slow. He'll be all right."

There was no way Max could guarantee that, but she clung to his words anyway. She dragged her hand through her hair. "Of course he will."

"We'll take my Land Rover. I've got a CB." He didn't have to add the words, "just in case." They both understood the dangers the wilderness held for a small boy alone.

Max exchanged a few words with Julia and another assistant, then climbed into the vehicle. Rikki was already sitting in it, waiting impatiently.

The sense of urgency going through her was hard to put into words, but she couldn't shake the feeling that time was of the essence. "The cave is due west."

Max started up the engine. "I know where the cave is."

There was no reason for the dig to take him to that section of her land. "How do you know?"

He flashed a small grin at her surprise as they sped away. "I used to play here as a kid. My property's adjacent to this place."

"The Ferguson place?" He had said "my." Rikki stared at him. "You *own* the Ferguson place?" It was a deserted piece of property that she hoped someday, if things went well, to be able to buy and add to her own.

"Yes." He glanced in her direction and could see all the questions multiplying in her head. "My dad bought that property from Lyle Ferguson over thirty years ago. But names have a tendency to stick around these parts. You still own the Baxter place."

Rikki shifted in her seat as they hit a rock. "I thought the bank owned the Ferguson place now."

"No, they own the note. I own the property." After his father had died, he couldn't bring himself to sell it. It had meant a lot to his father, so he had held on, letting the few remaining horses go. Now he was beginning to be glad he hadn't sold the property.

Another omission she had stumbled on by accident. Why hadn't he told her? Was there a reason why he hadn't wanted her to know the property belonged to him? "Why didn't you say anything before?"

Max shrugged. "I guess it never came up in conversation."

It was probably as simple as that. No secrets. Just no thought to the matter. Rikki gave in to the overwhelming impulse that came over her and punched him lightly in the arm.

He looked at her in surprise. "Just what was that for?"

"For not telling me." She folded her arms before her and stared straight ahead. "You have *got* to be the most closemouthed man I have *ever* met."

He laughed, and some of the tension drained out of her shoulders. "In my line of work, conversation isn't a necessary skill."

Perhaps not, but she had evidence to the contrary. "I've seen you with Elliot often enough. The two of you seem to talk up a storm when you're together. You've turned him into a regular chatterbox."

Max's smile softened as he thought of the boy. "Elliot's different. Special."

It pleased her that he felt that way. "Were you a loner, too?"

She could read between the lines, he thought. "Sort of."

"And lonely?" Had he been? Had it been as painful for him as it was for Elliot at times?

Elliot.

Oh Elliot, where are you?

She looked around impatiently, but all she could see was a sea of grass. They were quickly approaching the foothills. Elliot could be anywhere if he hadn't reached the cave.

"No, I was never lonely. I liked my own company."

Rikki's attention was drawn back to Max. A self-contained man. There was nothing she could offer him, she thought. He had his work, his dreams and his own company. He had everything he needed, everything he wanted. And he would be gone soon. She couldn't *make* him stay. That wouldn't be fair to either of them.

He saw the tension returning. It seemed to outline her entire body. "Worried?"

Rikki could feel her ears clogging as the Land Rover began to climb up the steep road. She grasped at the excuse he gave her, her thoughts returning to Elliot. "A little. He *is* only nine. A resourceful nine, but there are snakes and black widow spiders around here. And there are so many things that could happen to him."

"Don't think about it," Max advised. "I'm betting we'll find him none the worse for wear and excited about something he's discovered."

Her arms tightened around herself. She felt unaccountably cold, even though it was a warm day. "I'll take that bet. And I hope you win."

So do I, Rikki, so do I. Max kept his eyes on the road as the winding path narrowed even more.

After a few minutes of silence, she didn't want to be alone with her thoughts anymore. Her mind was wandering, her imagination working overtime. She needed the diversion of conversation if she was going to stay calm. "Why didn't you sell the property?"

Max felt the vehicle straining, even in low gear. Maybe they should have brought the horses. He shrugged in answer to her question. "Just a loose end I never got around to taking care of."

She studied his profile for a second, hoping to learn something from his expression that wasn't in his words. She didn't believe he really had "loose ends." The absentminded-professor image didn't fit anymore. "Is that the only reason?"

"No," he said slowly. "I guess I liked holding on to a piece of the past."

"The past again." Rikki was beginning to hate that word. It seemed to get in her way every time she turned around. An obstacle she couldn't seem to overcome.

Though he didn't often expose the more sentimental side of himself, he had a feeling Rikki would understand. "My dad loved the ranch. He bred horses, like you. Never quite made it, but he was happy, and I guess that's all that counts in the end."

"You loved him a lot." It wasn't a guess.

"Yes, I did. He was a little stern at times, but that was because he wanted the best for me. I didn't realize how hard it was for him to make a go of it." That realization had come later, after it was too late to say thank-you. "There were just the two of us."

"Your mother?" She knew that it was a very personal question, but they had gone beyond the boundary of mere polite conversation.

"Died when I was four. I barely remember her." It was one of the very few things he truly regretted. "My dad tried hard to make up for that." And in his own way, Max thought, his father had succeeded. He had never felt cold and alone when he was growing up. His father had always been there for him.

"You were lucky." Rikki couldn't help the wistful note in her voice.

He laughed. "One pair of shoes a year and hand-me-downs from a cousin in Salinas wouldn't be considered lucky by some."

The shoes and the clothes weren't important. They never had been to her. More of a prison than anything else. Her parents had always been obsessed with her wearing the right things, looking the right way, saying the right thing. There were other things, far more important, that created a child's sense of wealth or poverty. "I would have traded my life for yours. Gladly. There are memories in your eyes. Nice ones."

"Yes, they are at that. Maybe I hadn't realized just how nice they were until now. I couldn't wait to leave here. He died my first year in college. Emphysema. I didn't even know he was sick. He hadn't wanted me to know."

She doubted if Max's father had ancestors who'd docked at Plymouth Rock, as her mother did, or if his schooling had been even half as extensive as her father's. Certainly his money hadn't been. But she wished with all her heart that he had been her father instead of the man who was. "Sounds like quite a man."

"Yes, yes, he was."

And so was his son, she thought.

She looked ahead, and her thoughts returned to Elliot. Should they have brought more people with them after all? There were only two of them. How much ground could they cover if Elliot wasn't somewhere near the mouth of the cave? Doubts and apprehension began to resurface.

Max noticed the way she clenched her hands on her knees. She was almost rigid with tension. His conversation hadn't kept her mind off the reason they were there. He hadn't expected it to for long.

"Road ends here," he said unnecessarily, cutting off the engine. The Land Rover almost gasped with relief.

She was out in an instant. "The mouth of the cave is just on the other side." She pointed to it. They faced an even steeper incline than the one they had just come up.

He didn't want her getting hurt. "Look, why don't you stay here? I'll go up and see if—" He should have known better.

"The hell you will. I might not have grown up here, but that doesn't mean I can't climb. I'm not helpless."

"Have it your way." He knew he couldn't talk her out of coming. She was too stubborn for that. All he could do was follow and catch her if she fell. He grabbed a coil of rope from the back of the Land Rover and hurried to keep pace. Rikki was already walking toward the mouth of the cave. "How did you say Elliot knows about this place?"

My fault. It's my fault he's here. "I took him here last summer for a picnic. He has this ability to remember everything. Mind like a camera." She turned to look over her shoulder at Max and licked her lower lip. "If he's not here . . ."

"He'll be here."

The mouth of the cave was small. Rikki made it through easily, but Max had to crouch. It was not unlike the dig he'd gone on in South America last year, he thought. The memory made him shiver involuntarily.

Inside, the cave rose majestically some twenty feet above them, giving the appearance of an exceedingly large foyer. It measured some fifty feet or so across. But it quickly grew smaller, farther in, where there were several passageways leading off in different directions.

Rikki swung the flashlight in an arc around them, trying to illuminate the area. She had the mental image of being inside a bagpipe, a large inflated area with lots of small tubes protruding from it.

She bit her lower lip and looked at Max. "Which way?"

He nodded toward the tunnel closest to them. "We'll start with this one."

It was a dead end. The path quickly shrank to an opening less than two feet in diameter. Even Elliot wouldn't have been able to fit through that.

"One down," Max said, backing out.

To Rikki's relief, all the other tunnels proved to be equally impossible to negotiate. Except one. That one was long and winding, narrow but high enough for Max to walk without bending.

Rikki shone the light ahead of her. "Elliot?" The name was both a cry and a plea. She felt her throat tighten with fear and tears that wanted to surface. "Elliot, you'd better be here!" she cried, looking ahead of her. There was nothing to see but more tunnel.

Max noticed the sheen of sweat along her brow. It wasn't that hot in the cave. "What's the matter?" He could feel the fear rising from her.

"Nothing." She shook her head, waving away his concern. "Let's keep going."

He held her arm, anchoring her in place. "No, what is it?"

"It's stupid." She saw that he wasn't about to let her go until she explained. "I'm claustrophobic."

This was going to be too much for her. It was too much for him just watching her. "Then you shouldn't be here. Rikki, why don't you go back? I'll—"

Anger rose in her eyes. She wasn't about to be sent off just because she had a problem. It was hers, and she would handle it. There was too much at stake for her to give in. She'd known that when she had set out with Max. "No, he's my nephew. I'm going to bring him out of this cave. If he's here."

The last three words sounded more like a whispered prayer to Max.

"At least let me go ahead." Taking the flashlight from her, he led the way, holding her hand securely in his. His grip tightened as Rikki stumbled.

"Wait!" she cried, bending down to pick up what she had tripped over. "It's his backpack. He *is* here." Excited, Rikki moved ahead of Max. She could see the tunnel opening up a few feet away. "Elliot! Elliot, why don't you answer me?"

"Shh," Max warned. "Loud noises tend to do things in caves that we don't want to think about." The expedition in South America had ended in a cave-in. He had barely escaped alive.

Rikki pressed her lips together, trying to get a grip on her nerves. Why wasn't Elliot answering? He was here. He'd left his backpack. *Where was he?*

Impatient, Rikki moved ahead to the opening. She gasped, and Max grabbed her hand. She had almost walked off a ledge.

The floor of the cave dropped down not three feet away from where she stood. She couldn't see the bottom. Rikki's heart hammered in her throat. Without meaning to, her fingernails dug into Max's arm. She knew what his silence meant.

"No. He didn't. He couldn't have. I won't believe it!" Tears gathered in her eyes as she fought back the wave of hysteria that rose up in her throat. She could taste the bile in her mouth, the tinny flavor of fear.

Max held her to him. He couldn't find the words to comfort her. "Rikki, hush." He stroked her hair, holding her close.

She refused to let him comfort her. Elliot wasn't dead. He wasn't. She refused to accept that. She pulled away from the shelter of Max's chest, tottering slightly. Her arm was snaked around his as she looked down.

"Elliot!" A rumble in the distance answered her cry. Falling rocks. Rikki ignored the sound and the urgent tug on her arm. She wasn't going back without Elliot. "Elliot, answer me!"

She was going to start a cave-in. "Rikki," Max said compassionately, "he's not—"

"Shh!" She covered his mouth with her hand, cocking her head, trying to find the direction the sound had just come from. "Listen."

He pulled her hand away from his mouth. "What?" He didn't hear anything. Mercifully there were no more rocks falling. But they could only push luck so far.

"There it is again." She tugged on his shirt, trying to make Max hear. Her face turned back to his, her eyes growing bright with hope. "It's Elliot!"

"Aunt Rikki?" The cry was faint.

"Elliot. Elliot, where are you, honey?" She looked around frantically, but she couldn't see him.

"Here. Down here." The voice was hoarse, but clear.

Max grabbed her hand as she moved quickly past him. "His voice is coming from over there."

With her hand urgently clutching his, Max slowly made his way along the ledge as it narrowed even further. He shone the flashlight down. About seven feet below them ran a small jutting mantel of rock, only slightly wider than Elliot.

"I slipped," Elliot cried, squinting as the light hit him. His face was grimy with tears that had dried. "Pretty stupid, huh?"

"We'll discuss stupid later," Rikki said, her voice choking. "Let's get you out of here."

Max took the rope from his shoulder and uncoiled it. "I'm going to send down a rope, Elliot. You tie it around your waist and I'll pull you out."

"I can't."

The poor kid was probably scared to death, Max thought. "There's nothing to be afraid of, Elliot. I won't let you fall."

"No, I'm not afraid, Max." Rikki could hear the boy's voice tremble as he tried hard to be brave. "I broke my wrist. I can't move it."

Damn. "He won't be able to slip this around his waist even if I make a loop for him. I'm going to have to go down and get him."

The ledge looked as if it was hardly wide enough for Elliot. Max could never make it. If he tried, they both might fall. "It doesn't look wide enough to hold you. I'll go."

"Rikki—"

She couldn't afford to waste time arguing. "Look, I can pull Elliot up, but I can't support your weight. But you can hold me. You *will* hold me, won't you?" She turned her face up to his.

Every day of my life, if I can. "This is no time for jokes."

But she shook her head. "This is exactly the time for jokes." With fingers that shook slightly, she took the rope from him and tied one end around her waist. "I'm coming, Elliot. Hang on."

She held her breath as she took the first step down. The side was too smooth to give her anything to hold on to. Her fate was entirely in Max's hands. Inch by inch, he lowered her down. Rikki held on to the rough rope, afraid to let out a breath.

"Are you all right?" Max panted, his muscles quivering as tension gripped him, making every nerve ending alert.

The thundering noise in her ears was the sound of her own heart. "I don't think this is going to make it as the newest ride in Disneyland, but I'm okay."

It felt like an eternity before her feet touched the ledge and she could finally stand next to Elliot. A sob choked her when she looked at the boy. She didn't know whether to throw her arms around him and hold him close or shake him. There was no room to do either. And no time.

Elliot gave her a brave smile as he held his broken wrist with his other hand. She knew it had to hurt like the devil. Rikki wanted to do something to ease the pain, but first she had to get him out.

"C'mon, you're going for a ride." Fumbling slightly, Rikki untied the rope from around her waist and secured it around the boy's. She tugged slightly on the line. "Okay," she called up to Max. "Precious cargo coming up."

Max set the flashlight aside again in order to pull Elliot up. Because the boy was plunged into semidarkness, Max talked to him as he pulled. He had him more than halfway up when Max thought he heard a soft whistle floating up from the ledge.

"Rikki?" Max asked. "Is that you?"

She was trying not to think about the fact that she was standing in the dark on a ledge that could break away at any time and plunge her to her death. "Haven't you ever heard of whistling in the dark?"

Quickly he pulled Elliot to him, giving him a squeeze before removing the rope form his waist. "You did good, Elliot."

Nearing the edge again, Max shone the flashlight down to illuminate the ledge. "Would this be a good time to talk marriage?"

"This wouldn't be a good time to talk at all!" she cried. "Get me out of here."

Max set the flashlight near the edge and lowered the rope quickly. He passed the back of his wrist across his forehead, wiping away the sweat. "No bravado?"

"If you don't hurry up and get me, there'll be no *Rikki* in a minute." She gasped, her stomach quivering. "Something rough just brushed by my face."

"That's the rope. Feel it?"

She made a grab for it, pressing her back against the wall. Her heart was hammering in her chest so hard that she couldn't understand why it hadn't broken a rib yet. Somehow she managed to get the rope around her waist again. "Get me up, Max."

"With pleasure." She felt a tug and then slowly began to rise up in the air, her feet dangling below her. She heard Max groan. "You put on weight since I lowered you?"

"Max, get me up!"

Hand over hand, the rope ripping into his skin, Max pulled Rikki up until she was finally next to him. She gasped, dragging air into her constricted lungs. He wanted to hold her, to assure himself that she was all right.

Instead he turned to Elliot. "See, Elliot, you wait long enough, no telling what you can catch."

"Very funny." She scrambled to her feet, taking Elliot into her arms, being careful not to hurt his injured wrist. "We'll fix that as soon as we get you home," she promised.

Elliot collapsed against her shoulder, hugging her with his good arm. Tears wet her shirt. "I'm so sorry, Aunt Rikki."

She held him tightly, her own tears temporarily blinding her. "It's over and you're safe. That's all that matters, darling."

She looked at Max over the boy's head and mouthed, "Thank you."

Chapter Twelve

The reunion had been filled with raised voices, emotional embraces and tears. She couldn't recall ever seeing Virginia so concerned, so stripped of all the things that made her prideful and flighty, Rikki thought as she leaned forward to light the second candle on the dining room table. It looked as if it had finally dawned on her sister what being a mother was all about. In those few hours as she and her husband had helplessly waited to learn of Elliot's whereabouts, Virginia had grown. Rikki could see it in her eyes when Max entered, carrying Elliot in his arms.

Virginia and Wallace had fussed over Elliot's broken wrist as Rikki had set it. For a while Rikki had thought there was another argument in the making as to whose fault it all had been.

And then Max had put a stop to it.

Rikki yelped as the flame licked her fingertips, having burned its way up the match. Quickly she waved it out, then sighed. Max had surprised her.

He'd been masterful. She had felt and seen evidence of his strength, both literally and otherwise, all during the time they had been searching for Elliot. She had trusted Max not only with her life, but with Elliot's, as well, hanging on to that rope. She realized that she had never trusted anyone else so completely before.

Never loved anyone so completely before.

And then, after all the tension they had endured, when Virginia and Wallace were on the verge of casting the blame for the situation on each other, Max had effectively and simply cut through their rhetoric and made them see that they were wasting their entire lives, bogging themselves down in trivial matters. Elliot was alive, and they had a family to nurture before it died on the vine completely. Max made them suddenly see things differently, made them realize what an exceptional life they had.

Virginia had looked at Max with eyes that could finally see and quietly thanked him.

Imagine, Virginia humbled. It had been absolutely incredible to witness, Rikki mused, straightening the centerpiece she had fashioned with flowers from her garden. Wallace seemed to take the lead right before her eyes at that moment, telling Rikki that they would be going home now. *All* of them. As a family.

With his wife's hand in his, Wallace had turned to Elliot and asked his son if he was up to a vacation to the Grand Canyon. The answer had been a resounding yes. Dinosaurs, for the moment, had receded into the background.

It was going to be all right for them, she thought, satisfied. They were a family, possibly for the first time in

their lives. Rikki smiled. And Max had helped to make
it happen.

Max had made a lot of things happen. Rikki knew
now that she loved him. There was no getting around it.
Nor did she want to any longer. It wasn't because of the
way he kissed her. Though his tender passion burned
away her thoughts, she could still think clearly later. She
loved the man, dinosaurs and all. If they had differences, well, differences made people interesting. Besides, she told herself, they had more things in common
than not. And she wanted to spend the rest of her life
making it all mesh. If he would let her.

That was what this dinner was all about. Convincing
him. He had mentioned marriage when they were in the
cave, but she had no idea if he had only been joking. She
was determined to turn it into a serious matter.

She glanced at her watch. He would be here within
minutes. There wasn't much time. Rikki hurried back to
the bedroom to check herself over one last time. The
fourth "one last time."

The dress she had on was one her mother had selected for her a long time ago, when they had traveled to
France. If nothing else, Sondra McGuire had excellent
taste. Held up by the thinnest of straps, the soft turquoise dress rested lightly against Rikki like another
layer of skin, delicate, alluring, displaying curves in such
a way that temptation became a very tantalizing reality.

"He doesn't stand a chance," she told the reflection
in the bureau mirror, hoping fervently that she was right.

Except for the night of the party, Max had only seen
her in jeans and T-shirts. And even that had only been a
simple peasant outfit. On a scale of one to ten, that had
been a five. This was a twelve. She was a woman gear-
ing up for the one battle of the sexes she was deter-

mined to win. She was going to make him fall in love with her. Make him want her to be a part of his life forever. If that meant going with him on his digs, well, so be it. She wasn't so incomplete that she needed to define herself by an address. She hadn't realized that until this morning, in the cave, but she knew it now.

Her dark hair, brushed to a sheen, hung loose about her shoulders, inviting the touch of a man's hand.

At least, she hoped so.

The knock on the front door had her stomach muscles tightening.

"Show time," she murmured to herself. Smoothing the slightly flared petallike skirt against her hips, she went to answer the door.

Her nerves felt as if they were going to explode as she opened the door.

Max stared at her. She was a vision, a turquoise cloud swirling into his life, reducing everything else in her path to a meaningless blur. For a moment he couldn't move. He felt as if his knees were welded together. "Are we going out?"

"No." She held the door open wide, stepping back to admit him.

He looked inside. There didn't seem to be anyone else around. He knew that Virginia, Wallace and Elliot were gone. He had helped put their belongings into the car. "Is someone else coming?"

"No." She turned and led him to the dining room. He followed, mesmerized by the gentle way her hips were swaying. He wondered if she knew just how much restraint he was employing at this exact moment.

The dining room was dark except for the candles that flickered flirtatiously in the center of the table.

He was the first to admit that he was slow in certain matters, but he did catch on eventually. Max grinned. He stood behind his chair, leaning his hands on the back, drinking in the vision she made. "Are you trying to seduce me, Rikki?"

She had to remind herself that he was always honest. No beating around the bush for him. She fussed a little with the napkin at his place setting, a smile lifting the corners of her mouth. "Yes."

Max felt his breath catching every time he tried to exhale. "There's no point."

"Oh." There was no sign on his face of what he meant. Was he trying to find a polite way to let her down?

His eyes skimmed over her, noticing the way the fabric seemed to lightly dust her breasts, rising and falling when she breathed. Max gripped the chair harder. "You've already seduced me."

A warm feeling began to pour through her. It was all right. "When?"

"The first time I saw you standing in that doorway." He nodded toward the front door. He liked the way the light played upon her skin, turning it a golden color. He found himself wanting to make love to her by candlelight, by moonlight. And by no light at all. "Do you want to tell me what this is all about?"

As Rikki began to seat herself, Max crossed to her and pushed in the chair. Ever so lightly, he skimmed his fingers along her skin and watched her react.

Rikki turned, her cheek brushing against his hand. Her eyes fluttered shut for a moment; then she looked up at him. "You've already guessed."

"I guessed *what*. I didn't guess why." He moved back to his own chair.

"The why is obvious."

Max sat down, his eyes still on her. "Not to me. I'm dense. The absentminded professor, remember?"

Whatever there was to be said, to be understood between them, Max wanted to hear her say it, to hear the words from her lips. He'd never thought he would be the type to actually need words, but he did. This one time, he wanted it all perfectly clear. Who would ever have thought that of him?

Now that they were finally getting down to it, Rikki felt her nervous jitters returning. She wanted just a little more time. If she didn't ask, he couldn't say no. "Do you mind if we eat first?"

He looked down at the elaborate meal on his plate. It had taken her time to prepare this. A lot of time. "Why don't we eat and talk?"

"You always manage to get your way."

"No, I compromise. Compromise is the essence of survival. Of making things work."

And he had already made his compromises before he had come to her tonight.

Rikki suddenly realized that she had forgotten the butter.

"Need help?" Max asked as she rose from the table.

Rikki shook her head. "Just eat."

"That's what I do best." He watched her go into the kitchen. What was she up to? He knew what he wanted this to be about, but jumping to conclusions was not something he ever allowed himself to do. He preferred the slow and steady route. Except, perhaps, with her.

Max smiled broadly and waited for her to return.

"Rikki, the meal was heavenly. But we're up to dessert, and I don't want to talk about Virginia and Wallace, or even Elliot, anymore." He rose from the table and, crossing to her, took her hand.

A flash of insecurity swept through her. "The dishes—"

"Aren't going anywhere."

"No," she was forced to agree.

Rikki let him lead her to the sofa. When he sat down, she took a seat next to him, her hands folded in her lap like a child waiting to repeat her piece at a recital and be done with it.

No, not a child. A woman. Max longed to take her into his arms, to kiss her, to slip from her shoulders the straps that had been tantalizing him all through dinner and explore all the riches beneath.

He smiled to himself. Even at a time like this, he sounded like a paleontologist.

He reached over, took an icy hand into his and held it firmly. He looked into her eyes. "Talk."

They were soft, warm, friendly eyes, Rikki thought, studying them. Yet there was passion there. "I've been thinking."

"Yes?"

His voice was gentle, encouraging, and suddenly she wondered what she had been so nervous about. This was Max, Max who was the reason for everything, for the way she felt. The words tumbled out in a rush.

"I told you I wanted roots."

She was going to tell him why things couldn't work between them. She was trying to find a way to make him understand. Well, he wasn't about to understand that. Things *would* work. He opened his mouth to tell her that she no longer had to worry about leaving the ranch, but once she'd started, Rikki refused to stop.

She placed a hand on his chest. "No, let me finish. I never felt like I had roots before, and I only just now realized that I wasn't rootless because we moved from place to place. I was rootless because there wasn't anyone to love me while all the moving around was going on. My parents were always so concerned with images that they never bothered to look beneath the surface, never bothered to get to know me, to understand what it was I wanted, what I *needed*. Love would have given me roots." She smiled at him. "Love has. I don't need the ranch anymore. I need you."

He'd been worried for no reason. Max grinned. "You might not need the ranch, but I do."

She didn't understand. "What?"

"They found more fossils in both sites while we were out looking for Elliot. My dinosaur is definitely here on your property, and it looks like we may be here for a long, long time." He leaned back, one arm hooked around the back of the sofa. "Some digs go on for years, you know."

And from the way he said it, she could see that he intended for this one to go on that long.

"'We,'" she repeated. "As in you and your crew?"

She was being coy. On her, it was definitely stirring. He let her have her moment. "I was thinking more in terms of a smaller 'we,' as in you and I."

"Oh," she said, pleased.

"Yes, 'oh.'" He shook his head at the wonder of it all. "You know, I feel a little like Dorothy, clicking her heels together and murmuring, 'There's no place like home.'"

He was a very large Dorothy. Rikki laughed at the image. "The ruby slippers wouldn't fit."

"No, but the rest of it does," he added, growing serious. "I've been to all four corners of the earth, searching. Who would ever have thought that the one great find of my life would be right here in my own backyard?''

"Do you really think there's a whole dinosaur down there?''

He pulled her closer to him. "I wasn't talking about the dinosaur."

"Oh?" This time, there was wonder in her eyes. He would never get tired of looking into those eyes, Max thought. Violet had quickly become his favorite color.

"I was talking about you," he said softly. "Say 'oh' again."

She looked at him, puzzled. "Why?"

"Because when you do, you purse your lips."

"Is that good?"

"I don't know about good," he said as he trailed the back of his hand along her cheek, "but it is very, very sexy." Max buried his hands in her hair as he drew her face close to his. "You know, you'd make a pretty good paleontologist yourself."

No, things were definitely not predictable around him. "Where did that come from?"

"You managed to dig out a part of me that I had no idea was there." A small smile played over his lips as he remembered. "A part that I was specifically informed *wasn't* there."

Rikki's brows drew together. "Sally again?" It was a good thing the woman had moved out of town. Rikki didn't think she could trust herself around Sally if she still lived in Senora.

Max shook his head slowly, still framing her face. "Sally never again. Only you." Softly he kissed her, then drew back.

She had expected more. Feeling confused, she looked at him. "So, what are your plans?"

"You really want to know?"

"Yes." She saw a mischievous smile taking hold, showing her the boy he once was.

"Got a minute?"

Rikki cocked her head, regarding him with a teasing look in her eyes. "Is that how long it will take?"

"No." He nudged her over and settled her onto his lap, tangling one finger in the strap farthest from him. "As a matter of fact, what I have in mind is going to take all night."

The warmth began to rush through her again. "Funny you should mention that. I just happen to have all night."

Ever so slowly, he pressed a kiss to her shoulder. "Did I mention that I love you?"

"No," she breathed, settling her hands around his neck. "Mention it."

He looked into her face. "I do. I think I probably knew all along, but it came to me in the cave, when I watched your head disappear from view over the edge and I thought to myself, what if I never saw you again? What if you disappeared from my life? I couldn't stand it. I couldn't let that happen. I love you, Dr. Erikka McGuire."

With his hands skimming along her bare skin that way, it was hard to keep her mind on words. "Oh, we're getting formal. I guess this is official, then."

He kissed her shoulder again, his mouth slipping lower as the fabric dipped, before he answered. "As official as you want."

Her eyes opened wide as she savored the moment. "Then you're talking marriage?"

"That's the official I had in mind."

She laughed, imagining the triumph in Virginia's face when she told her. "Virginia will be very happy."

"How about you?"

She looked down into his face in a way that totally unsettled and disarmed him. "You have to ask?"

He took a breath, her scent filling his soul. "No, I guess I don't."

She shivered as his fingers began to play with the second strap. "As I recall, you mentioned something about 'all night'?"

Max kissed the hollow of her throat, feeling the pulse there quiver beneath his lips. "I don't want to talk anymore."

"Funny, neither do I."

*   *   *   *   *

SMYTHESHIRE, MASSACHUSETTS.

Small town. Big secrets.

Silhouette Romance invites you to visit Elizabeth August's intriguing small town, a place with an unusual legacy rooted deep in the past. . . .

THE VIRGIN WIFE (#921) February 1993
HAUNTED HUSBAND (#922) March 1993
LUCKY PENNY (#945) June 1993
A WEDDING FOR EMILY (#953) August 1993

Elizabeth August's SMYTHESHIRE, MASSACHUSETTS—
This sleepy little town has plenty to keep you up at night.
Only from Silhouette Romance!

Take 4 bestselling love stories FREE

Plus get a FREE surprise gift!

Special Limited-time Offer

Mail to Silhouette Reader Service™

3010 Walden Avenue
P.O. Box 1867
Buffalo, N.Y. 14269-1867

YES! Please send me 4 free Silhouette Romance™ novels and my free surprise gift. Then send me 6 brand-new novels every month, which I will receive months before they appear in bookstores. Bill me at the low price of $1.99* each plus 25¢ delivery and applicable sales tax, if any.* That's the complete price and—compared to the cover prices of $2.75 each—quite a bargain! I understand that accepting the books and gift places me under no obligation ever to buy any books. I can always return a shipment and cancel at any time. Even if I never buy another book from Silhouette, the 4 free books and the surprise gift are mine to keep forever.

215 BPA AJH5

Name	(PLEASE PRINT)	
Address	Apt. No.	
City	State	Zip

This offer is limited to one order per household and not valid to present Silhouette Romance™ subscribers.
*Terms and prices are subject to change without notice. Sales tax applicable in N.Y.

USROM-93R ©1990 Harlequin Enterprises Limited

Is your father a Fabulous Father?

Then enter him in Silhouette Romance's

"FATHER OF THE YEAR" Contest
and you can both win some great prizes! Look for contest details
in the FABULOUS FATHER titles available in June, July
and August . . .

ONE MAN'S VOW by Diana Whitney
Available in June

ACCIDENTAL DAD by Anne Peters
Available in July

INSTANT FATHER by Lucy Gordon
Available in August

Only from

**Relive the romance...
Harlequin and Silhouette
are proud to present**

by Request

A program of collections of three complete novels by the most
requested authors with the most requested themes. Be sure to
look for one volume each month with three complete novels by
top name authors.

In June: **NINE MONTHS** Penny Jordan
                                    Stella Cameron
                                    Janice Kaiser

**Three women pregnant and alone. But a lot can
happen in nine months!**

In July: **DADDY'S**   Kristin James
             HOME   Naomi Horton
                              Mary Lynn Baxter

**Daddy's Home... and his presence is long
overdue!**

In August: **FORGOTTEN**   Barbara Kaye
           PAST   Pamela Browning
                           Nancy Martin

**Do you dare to create a future if you've forgotten
the past?**

Available at your favorite retail outlet.

HARLEQUIN   Silhouette